Henry Nutter

Local Rhymes

Henry Nutter

Local Rhymes

ISBN/EAN: 9783337260996

Printed in Europe, USA, Canada, Australia, Japan

Cover: Foto ©Andreas Hilbeck / pixelio.de

More available books at **www.hansebooks.com**

BY

HENRY NUTTER,

BURNLEY.

BURNLEY:
B. MOORE, "GAZETTE" PRINTING WORKS, BRIDGE STREET.
1890.

PREFACE.

THE following songs and poems have appeared from time to time in the *Burnley Gazette*. The author, not deeming them worthy of more than a passing notice, never intended placing them before the public in any other way; but in consequence of the interest taken in a few of the pieces, he has considered it his duty to publish them in the present cheap form. This little volume contains poems written chiefly on local topics, and can therefore be of little interest except to those readers who have some acquaintance with the circumstance or subject of each piece.

Yours truly,

HENRY NUTTER.

LOCAL POEMS.

—o—

TO MR. H. HOULDING, BURNLEY.

Hail! sweetest poet of the Brun,
To you these heartfelt lines are spun ;
Long may your kind autumnal sun
      Keep bright and clear,
And safely through its orbit run
      For many a year.

My dear old minstrel, tell me why
Your Muse of late has been so shy ?
While in peculiar metre I
      Dare touch the strings :
Or with spasmodic efforts fly
      On broken wings.

This minor bard has long revered
The poet who has nobly steered
A faithful pen ; while cowards feared
      A soul so brave :
Long may his patriarchal beard
      In honour wave !

Your Muse, my friend, is sweet and true ;
I've read the volume sent by you,
With growing interest through and through,
      My reverend sire ;
And find each time more credit due
      To your sweet lyre.

Your notes are touched with graceful ease
Their modulated numbers please
Like zephyrs playing through the trees
     " In Summer Days ; "
With tuneful pure Parnassian breeze
     You pour your lays.

Then come, dear Houlding, strike your lyre,
And like the soaring lark aspire ;
Or to your favourite shades retire
     Among the woods,
And join the cheerful feathered choir
     By Calder's floods.

Sing gently your sweet " Song of Rest,"
Or read to me of " Pendle's " crest,
Or " Walks in Snow " where children pressed
     Their " tiny feet : "
Or " By the River " which you blessed
     With musings sweet.

In " Summer Skies " and " Moonrise " eves,
When " In the Woods " your fancy weaves,
" Forget-me-nots," and " Autumn Leaves "
     " In Peace "; and " Rest,"
" Friendship " to " The Soul's Answer " cleaves
     In " Wild Flowers " dressed.

Come then your humble friend to greet ;
Leave every proof and leader sheet,
And that hard Editorial seat,
     And darksome ink :
In bowers ambrosial let us meet,
     And nectar drink.

I, like the simple robin sing,
The last in autumn, first in spring ;
At dusk or dawn, with shivering wing
    I chant along :
To you I dedicate and bring
    This simple song.

The critic may such lines despise,
And carping look profoundly wise :
His scowling deep tempestuous eyes
    May roll away :
He harms me not, he may chastise,
    But cannot slay.

With pen from fear or favour loose,
The honest critic must conduce
To raise the poet's aim and use
    Whom he assails :
If free from bias, or abuse,
    He holds the scales.

But if his tooth be piercing sharp,
And badger bound in woof and warp,
He then in vain may carve and carp,
    And cast his sting :
He cannot silence one sweet harp,
    Or break a string.

My Muse is now on danger's brink ;
For suddenly I pause : and think,
That *you* have scribbled critic's ink,
    And acid too,
And made artistic authors shrink,
    And tremble through.

When to your strictures I allude,
I feel I'm from my latitude :
No further now will I intrude
   Upon your time,
But right or wrong I thus conclude
   This simple rhyme.

TO MR. GEORGE CROMPTON, VIOLINIST, LAUND.

This simple scroll in haste I've penned
To you, my genial fiddler friend ;
More faithful lines no man can send
   In your direction ;
To them your kind attention lend
   And keen inspection.

This week, alas ! I heard again
That you for days in bed had lain
With that accurst rheumatic pain,
   Which sorely lingers ;
Still worse : I heard that it had slain
   Your left hand fingers.

Good heavens, said I, those tuneful claws,
Which mark the quaver, breve and pause,
And timely answer when he draws
   The glorious bow—
No more will win the loud applause,
   The electric flow.

Those limbs could nimbly fly, or creep,
And true as nature, time could keep,
Attendant on the rapturous sweep
   Of your fleet hand,
Which drew the heart-transporting cheep
   With sure command.

My thoughts that instant flew upon
Beethoven, Handel, Mendelssohn
And Spohr : musicians gone
  To heaven safe—
And Crowther, Nelson, Titherington,
  John Booth and Scaife.

And then I breathed this fervent prayer ;
May heaven these tuneful fiddlers spare ;
And your old nimble *claws* repair
  And guiding thumb,
That I your pleasing notes may share
  For years to come.

Just when this heartfelt prayer I heaved
And to your case my soul had cleaved,
I from the postman's hand received
  A welcome letter,
Announcing (what my heart relieved),
  That you were better.

As sure as Irish eggs are eggs
And fiddlers to their neighbours plagues,
At once I sprung upon my legs
  And spread my wings ;
Then seized my fiddle, screwed his pegs,
  And touched the strings.

I thought of dear old Jubal's lyre,
And raised the pitch a little higher ;
Then English hornpipes went like fire,
  And Irish jigs,
And Scottish airs that you admire,
  With Barley Rigs.

On Jack's the Lad,' my heart went wild,
Then reels and polkas quick were filed,
My wife cried, Harry ! draw it mild,
        That wicked fiddle :
" I thought I was again a child,"
        With lightsome diddle.

Then on to Cambria's hills and dells :
My bow of Harlech's March oft tells,
And sweet Ash Grove in cadence swells
        Its joyful tones—
With Aberdovy's dear old bells,
        And Jenny Jones.

Through my poor scraping tweedling faults,
My graceless bow in lilts and waltz,
Makes bars by various slips and vaults,
        Inconstant roll :
And yet the sound my heart exalts,
        Or soothes my soul.

The happy fiddler's matchless art
In nature plays a glorious part ;
With magic bow quick as a dart
        He sweeps the strings,
And near with joy the human heart,
        To heaven he brings !

His soul-inspiring dexterous skill,
Draws out the charming notes at will,
Sweet as the throstle's purest trill
        Or linnets gay,
Whose songs the verdant valleys fill
        In merry May.

And then, what joy his art promotes
When his enchanted bow devotes
Its power to strike staccata notes,—
    Those brilliant sparks,
Like warblings from the happy throats
    Of soaring larks.

While nature health and strength affords,
Oh ! may your fingers gauge the chords,
To draw from old Cremona boards
    The scale chromatic,
And sweetly play like April birds,
    With bow emphatic.

All hail, ye tuneful fiddlers then !
The heart and ear direct my pen,
No sorrow is so deep as when
    The fiddlers fall :
The happiest souls possessed by men,
    Are fiddlers all.

THE NEW BOROUGH OF NELSON.

Tune : "St. Patrick was a Gintleman."

Come, listen to my simple song with patience
    and attention ;
Keep silent every restless tongue while here
    with joy I mention
That Nelson is my glorious theme—her charter,
    brief, and story—
Her municipal borough scheme, in all its coming
    glory.

Chorus :
Success to Nelson's Council Board, her
        Aldermen, and Mayor ;
That they may live in sweet accord, is our
        united prayer.

This day with cheerful hearts we toast the
        Nelson Corporation
(And England of that name will boast long as
        the earth's duration) ;
Though honours high are on her piled, in
        meritorious stages,
She is but yet a budding child to bloom in
        future ages.
                Success to Nelson's, &c.

Young Nelson boasts an upright trade in all
        her various classes ;
Her matchless   fancy goods are made by
        Nelson's bonny lasses,
Her brilliant spots and gay sateens adorn each
        local heiress,
Her fine jeanettes and lovely jeans would grace
        a Nelson Mayoress.
                Success to Nelson's, &c.

Your sixteen squares are full or more, without
        the least disguising,
Where every inch counts sixty-four, of sterling
        counts comprising ;
Thus merchants get their proper dues, goods are
        what you define them,
And Oldham's honest thirty-twos are just as
        they consign them.
                Success to Nelson's, &c.

From right your tradesmen never flinch, sound
 principles impel them,
Their warp and weft in every inch are truly as
 they sell them.
These truths are clear, which I record, with
 your entire permission,
No agent ever doubts their word, or charges
 imposition.
 Success to Nelson's, &c.

The Queen that wears the British crown has
 granted you a charter,
The reason is that Nelson town is sound in
 every quarter ;
Then cast away all care and gloom, throughout
 the coming winter,
And may you clear in every loom, a shilling on
 each printer.
 Success to Nelson's, &c.

Expand your wings, ye sage-like Board, in
 neighbourly alliance,
But take not dear old Barrowford without her
 full compliance.
The lovely vale might joy reflect with her
 green banks and bowers,
Her generous heart and intellect would raise
 your mental powers.
 Success to Nelson's, &c.

Her stately piles of ancient halls would throw
 a lustre o'er you,
Her healing springs and waterfalls would dance
 with joy before you !

The banks of Hutherstone would ring with
　　　stock-doves sweetly cooing,
Above the groves where maidens sing when
　　　lovers fond are wooing.
　　　　　Success to Nelson's, &c.

Include fair rosy Brierfield, and lovely Reedley
　　　Hallows,
Then charming Wheatley Lane would yield,
　　　which Pendle Forest follows ;
Spen Brook and Thornyholme you'll take
　　　without the slightest parley,
And for your future honour's sake include
　　　Newchurch and Barley.
　　　　　Success to Nelson's, &c.

Take calm Roughlee, the boggarts' lair, where
　　　witches walked abroad in,
And Blacko bright, and Foulridge fair, and
　　　Laneshawbridge and Trawden,
And bonny Colne, which monarchs prized and
　　　poured their blessings on her ;
Although you think she's fossilized, she still
　　　maintains her honour.
　　　　　Success to Nelson's, &c.

On ancient charters do not trench, for these she
　　　takes a pride in ;
On her impartial County Bench stern justice
　　　sits deciding ;
For these prerogatives she'll fight, Nelsonians
　　　may rest on ;
She must maintain her sacred right, of sending
　　　roughs to Preston.
　　　　　Success to Nelson's, &c.

Her dear old church and charming bells, with
    their associations,
The organ's diapason swells, with pious
    intonations,
Are sweet and sacred to the town by filial true
    affection ;
To take in Colne with her renown would be a
    sad reflection.
        Success to Nelson's, &c.

Let Nelson still discreetly reign, and hold what
    she possesses ;
In honour's path she'll yet obtain far more
    sublime successes.
Her borders still may she extend, may all her
    works be thorough,
And at the next Reform Bill send a member for
    the borough.
        Success to Nelson's, &c.

Old Burnley sends her love by me, and tenders
    you her greeting ;
From jealous feelings we are free at this your
    charter meeting ;
Wide may your borough still expand by well
    directed labour,
Till Burnley grasps you by the hand a close and
    friendly neighbour.
        Success to Nelson's, &c.

For Nelson's Council thus we'll pray, in love
    and faith fraternal ;
May heaven bless their lives each day, their sins
    forgive nocturnal !

Long may your lads be strong and true, in
    honour's path abiding
And Nelson's bonny lasses you, be cautious in
    deciding !
        Success to Nelson's, &c.

Accept a simple poet's prayer, each Nelson saint
    and sinner,
May every local magnate there, enjoy the
    chairman's dinner :
My pen I now lay on the shelf, and feel a little
    slighted ;
I should have dinnered there myself, but never
    Gott invited !

ANSWER TO AN INVITATION TO DINNER.

My esteemed Mr. Gott, I could see through the
    plot,
    On receiving your kind invitation ;
So I summoned my Muse, and she bade me
    refuse
    To attend on the present occasion.

Though my heart was relieved, when your card
    I received,
    With its neat little garland of beauty ;
'Twas a dear golden wreath, with a motto
    beneath,
    Saying " Nelson, this day do your duty."

Don't regard me remiss, in refusing the bliss
    Of enjoying your dinner and laughter ;
Yet it surely is wise, and a fair compromise
    If I turn in a few minutes after.

But alas ! if you think, there's a crack in one link
   In the chain of a friendship I cherish ;
I reply there is not, and I swear by my *Gott*
   That a friendship like ours cannot perish !

ADDRESS TO MR. TATTERSALL WILKINSON, ANTIQUARIAN.

Dear Wilkinson, old antiquarian friend,
   Of deep philosophical powers,
Whose lectures on science I often attend
   In winter's dark, tedious hours :
Your knowledge is vast, and your faculties great,
   False teaching through life you've eschewed,
Yet do not on subjects sidereal dilate,
   But keep in your own latitude.

In realms of antiquity revel at will
   On your ghastly mission alone,
Delve up your old cists with sepulchral skill,
   Till you find the philosopher's stone.
Root out and unearth some pre-Adamite limb,
   Flint implements, bronzes and jars,
Find bones of your ancestors, darksome and grim;
   But shun the bright planets and stars.

Unchronicled facts are discovered and solved
   By relics that you have amassed ;
Go on and reveal when our parents evolved
   From anthropoid stems of the past.
Dig out the small skulls from the tombs of your
      sires,
   Examine their thickness and size,
All calcined with antediluvian fires,
   But look not, my friend, to the skies.

Lay bare the mysterious tumulous mound,
    With shrewd antiquarian pains ;
There archæological wonders are found,
    And primeval human remains.
These ancient progenitors calmly exhume,
    And in your weird mission exult ;
Uncover with reverence each primitive tomb,
    But touch not the star-spangled vault.

From times pre-historic to Adam you come,
    To Nimrod, and Jacob, and Job ;
Through Babylon, Nineveh, Athens, and Rome,
    To recent events on this globe.
Your tales of antiquity I can commend,
    Your style is attractive and free,
Then stick to terrestrial matters, my friend,
    And leave stellar subjects to me.

REPLY TO THE ANTIQUARIAN.
INTERCEPTED LETTER.
TO THE EDITOR.

Some verses from a friend I saw
In your *Gazette*, four days ago ;
An answer quick indeed I owe
    To his petition :
So here is my reply below,
    With your permission.

I would not for the world offend
My noble antiquarian friend,
But to his prayer at once attend
    Without refusal :
The simple lines enclosed I send
    For his perusal.

Hail mighty chief of ancient urns !
Who prehistoric tombs discerns,
And in yon haunted vale sojourns
    With ghostly notion ;
And cists and calcined bones upturns
    With weird devotion.

Your kindly tuneful lines I've read,
And shuddered at the life you've led
Among the dark primordial dead,
    Without complaining :
Where dismal mounds are grimly spread,
    Old bones containing.

What find you there to entertain
Your highly convoluted brain,
In delving up with might and main
    What death embraces ?
How dare you touch with hands profane
    Those sacred places ?

It seems malicious, vile and strange,
Amid sepulchral scenes to range,
As if you sought an interchange
    With some dark shade,
Or spiteful thirsted for revenge
    Among the dead.

Now just suppose (I humbly crave)
That some old antiquarian gave
A hungry look upon your grave,
    With spade in hand :
Why, man ! you'd tremble, curse and rave,
    And shake the land !

Pray leave those jars and calcined bones
Where dim departed echo moans,
And grasp the earth's wide circular zones
            Or solar sphere :
Then soar aloft to starry thrones,
            And revel there.

Mark Mercury's wild rapid flight,
Watch Venus—lovely Venus bright,
And valiant Mars, in ruddier light,
            Who rolls serene,
With isles and continents in sight
            In verdure green.

Away to Jupiter my friend,
His belts and moons pray comprehend,
To Saturn's glorious rings then bend
            With love and praise :
Uranus and to Neptune lend
            Your wondering gaze.

Dig deep in yon star-spangled vault,
Through depths and heights, nor weary halt !
Though doubts and fears thy faith assault,
            They cannot sever
Thy mind from themes that must exalt
            Thy soul for ever.

No perils shall thy heart despond
Through deep sidereal space beyond
Where distant triple stars are donned
            In bright array ;
All gravitating in one bond
            They roll away.

Behold our winter nights display,
The brilliant constellations gay,
Orion's belt, the Milky Way,
       Those vapoury shrouds ;
Then near the Southern Cross survey
       Magellan's clouds.

Could you each constellation trace
When viewing heaven's starry face,
All single stars and every brace,
       With happy soul ;
You there would revel deep in space,
       From pole to pole.

But still you get a feeble glance
Of yonder boundless wide expanse,
Where suns in countless millions dance,
       With worlds around :
In billions more as you advance,
       They still abound.

And pray, thou mighty man of jars,
Why ask of solar spectrum bars ?
Although there be canals in Mars,
       And urns ! my friend :
There surely are no farthest stars,
       They have no end.

For when the keen observer plies
His powerful lense to sweep the skies,
Where unknown galaxies arise
       In numbers vast ;
Still on imagination flies
       To regions past.

On every side, from every place,
No mind can grasp, no eye can trace,
No numbers count, no words embrace
　　　　The infinite scroll:
No end to stars, no end to space,
　　　　Alas my soul!

Then from your mouldering bones get free,
With doubtful ghastly pedigree,
And sweep yon starry vault with me
　　　　With lightsome heart:
Celestial wonders bright we'll see,
　　　　And never part.

No jealous feelings here you'll find;
As Shakespeare writes of human kind
That dark suspicion haunts the mind
　　　　Of guilty man;
Sublunar things we'll leave behind
　　　　For fools to scan.

We envy not the worldly wise
Who never raises his dull eyes
To fields, where suns in distant skies
　　　　Their rays unfold;
But grovelling on the earth still lies
　　　　Scratching for gold.

Then bid farewell to urns and cists,
Your humble friend at once insists;
Go sell your jars to alchemists
　　　　With wizard dreams:
And leave your dismal swamps and mists
　　　　For loftier themes.

THE ASTRONOMER'S REPLY TO THE ANTIQUARIAN'S SECOND LETTER.

Dear friend of antiquarian fame,
Whose love fraternal here I claim,
As thus with pride in rhyme I name
      Your heavenly vision,
Which, when I read, at once I came
      To this decision.

I thought your bugle sounded truce,
That you had slipped the stellar noose,
And vowed when you had broken loose
      From yonder stars,
That no man should again seduce
      You from your jars.

But this is folly I perceive,
For which your humble friend will grieve ;
Suppose you get a short reprieve
      For recreation ;
Before you take a final leave,
      Or observation.

I like your poem, the latter part
Is really written from the heart ;
You quote the scripture for a start,
      My pious friend :
And ring the chords with tuneful art
      On to the end.

Although your verses made me vain,
I've fallen to myself again ;
I'm free from envy, pride and pain
      As any mortal ;
Or like you in your dreamy strain
      At heaven's portal.

The music of the minor bard,
At times receives the heart's reward :
He sings away without regard
      To cold disdain :
The cruel critics ne'er retard
      His cheerful strain.

Your tender feelings well I know—
Your bosom's gentle overflow—
To those who suffer here below,
      You're not afraid
To soothe, and pity, and to throw
      Your kindly aid.

With wealth of knowledge still in store,
Sing on, great chief of ancient lore ;
Of eastern battles by the score,
      In bygone ages,
In Nimrod's days, and long before
      The Hebrew sages.

Tell, in thy clear harmonious strains,
Of plundering hordes, and mad campaigns,
In Egypt, Troy, on Chaldean plains,
      And Spain's arena ;
Down from the ark thy mind retains
      To Navarino.

Deep-versed in ancient Greece and Rome
In prehistoric lore at home,
Through pyramids thy fancies roam
      To Pharoah's cellar ;
From Babel's tower to Caesar's tomb
      And Pompey's pillar.

To history's page, your mind is prone,
For proofs you stand unmatched, alone,
Each jar, and cist, and calcined bone
      Your spade's uphurled,
Your buck-horn needles, bronze and stone,
      Defy the world.

Look up to yonder blue abyss,
All former sympathies dismiss :
Those stars are matter, simply this,
      Thou man of lore,
And indestructible it is
      For evermore !

Some people think it matters not,
And never seem to care a jot,
How worlds are made, or where they're got;
      Oh wondrous theory !
But grant me just a parting shot
      Upon this query.

Let prejudice no truth evade,
Think and ask how worlds are made—
How they kindle, how they fade,
      And how they die !—
Why meteors nightly cannonade,
      And blaze on high !

No mortal can one tittle add
To matter, either good or bad ;
Though matter in all forms is clad,
      In boundless space,
It never a beginning had,
      In time or place.

In yonder spread of suns afar,
There is at times a stellar war;
And though self luminous they are,
    As you well know,
At once some dimly-glittering star
    Will brighter glow.

In scenes like these stars may collide,
As on through space they swiftly glide;
In all directions, far and wide,
    They fiercely meet,
And quickly melt, and then abide
    In fervent heat.

These rolling suns, this wondrous mass
Is thus once more reduced to gas,
And must to smaller compass pass,
    By radiation;
Ten million years are spent, alas!
    In condensation.

The awful term of years must run
Before the blazing future sun
Has from its surface, one by one,
    The planets cast—
The process must keep moving on
    Until the last.

The atoms of this gaseous cloud
Would, in condensing, closer crowd:
A rolling ball, thus, boiled aloud
    Our infant planet,
Until the cosmoplastic shroud
    Cooled into granite.

The cooling planets all, of course,
Move on by centrifugal force,
Around the great attractive source
   From which they flew ;
This theory you may not endorse,
   But yet 'tis true.

As on they roll, there surely must
In cooling down be formed a crust,
Which men of science don't distrust,
   Though fools have jeered ;
Some say how life evolved, and just
   When it appeared.

The rocks that lie above, in turn,
Were from the beds of granite worn :
Then by the sweeping floods were borne
   To boiling seas,
Where lava streams, rocks split and torn
   Were mixed with these.

Thus all the higher seams we know,
Are made from neighbour rocks below,
And fossil shapes of life there flow
   In changing swarms,
Where species, still evolving, show
   Improving forms.

When man appeared we'll leave it o'er,
As we have often done before ;
Henceforth I'll love you more and more
   Where e'er you rove ;
You're welcome ever to explore
   The skies above.

The truce is ended, peace is made,
Then roam away, where angels tread ;
Yea, soar aloft to scenes o'er head
    Among the stars ;
Or deeper dig among the dead
    For flint and jars.

REPLY TO H. BURROWS.

Dear Burrows, the verses you recently sent
    To the Radical paper of Burnley,
Were tunefully numbered and tenderly meant,
    Though critics may grin and look sternly.

This answer accept, with the heartiest thanks,
    Of him in whose honour you wrote them ;
Yet as for his random and doggerel pranks
    Few people I trow ever note them.

Though on my poor rhymes your opinion is
    wild !
    A thoughtless and strange observation :
So please, my dear Burrows, henceforth draw
    it mild,
    And lower your false estimation.

The few puny lines, with their meteor glow,
    That I write with a desperate muster,
Of service may be, as a contrast, to show
    The change from a great poet's lustre.

My sails to the undermost current are spread,
    My warbling at best is a wailing,
My efforts may touch not the heart or the head,
    Yet still the sweet Muse I keep hailing.

Great Browning and Swinburne are brilliant
    lights,
And merit the laurels they're wearing,
And Tennyson, too, with his loftiest flights
    His greatness is seen by comparing.

In sounding our simple unmusical drones,
    For which toothy cavillers blame us ;
We add to the splendour and sweeten the tones
    Of poets whose talents are famous.

The thief (though a rascal) makes honesty shine,
    The lazy exalts the industrious,
The sinks of iniquity blindly combine
    To make spotless virtue illustrious.

Then let us sing on for the sake of the great,
    To give them a broader foundation ;
The baser our notes, and the higher their state ;
    Let this be our justification.

The snarler who censures us vainly assails,
    Though proud of his learned authority,
We pay no regard to his measures and scales,
    But sing for the simple minority.

Content let us write in our doggerel ways,
    There surely is nothing else for us ;
In the vale of the Brun we will mumble our lays,
    My dear brother sinner H. Burrows.

AN ANSWER TO THE MAYOR'S INVITATION TO DINNER.

My dear Mr. Mayor, you may take it for granted,
Your card is most welcome ; 'tis just what I
    wanted ;
My Muse must reply, so at once I invoke her,
And dream of my swallow-tail coat and white
    choker.

Your kind invitation is freely accepted,
And doubtless this answer is what you expected ;
So here is my promise, I'll come if I can, sir,
My palate spontaneously echoes the answer.
When dining with friends of a generous nature,
I'm at peace with the world, sir, and every
          creature.
With scents aromatic my head well anointed,
I'll come at the time that the mayor has
          appointed.

With an appetite fairly well sharpened and keen,
The attendant will instantly ken what I mean,
To your dinner although I shall joyfully bend,
'Tis a trifle compared to mine host and a friend.
With friendship so genial I'm truly content,
Of my home and surroundings I make no
          complaint.
The old rocks at my feet are all sermons to me
In proclaiming the line of a long pedigree.

The moon, with her craters, her mountains and
          plains,
With pleasure I note as she waxes and wanes ;
Dear Venus and Jupiter, Saturn and Mars,
Are neighbours compared to the far distant stars;
These planets I tell, and with reverence I halt,
And gaze with delight on the star-spangled vault;
The grand constellations that glitter above,
Their outlines I trace with amazement and love,
As nightly my thoughts on their grandeur repose,
Each star is a wonder to me as it glows ;
As seasons advance, their positions I trace,
And shrink at the thought of an infinite space,
Where numberless millions of systems extend,
Assembled in galaxies, worlds without end ;

Immeasurably deep, inconceivably vast,
With firmaments boundless, the mind stands
    aghast.
All figures are useless that man has employed,
To number the stars, or encompass the void ;
No eye can distinguish or mind penetrate
To fathom their distance, connection or state.
Still deeper I trow where no telescope probes,
Are centres of systems with comets and globes.
Good heavens ! dear Greenwood, our merciful
    mayor,
You see no connection with dinners out there.
This dear little planet that flies round the sun,
With Burnley, the pride of the Calder and Brun,
Is dearer to you for the future by far,
Than sun, moon, or Venus, or comet, or star.
In local statistics you've reason to boast,
With subjects sublunar your mind is engrossed,
But here let my wandering Muse make a pause
And bring these unmusical lines to a close ;
Your patience I've wearied with this silly rhyme,
But hope to be with you next Friday in time.

ON THE MARRIAGE OF
MR. CHARLES WHITTLE AND MISS
MARY BOND, BURNLEY.

Dear Mary, you tender your freedom this day,
    You sacrifice body and purse ;
Then be not rebellious, but love and obey,
    And take him for better *and* worse.

A nervous sensation creeps over my skin,
    That some of your friends must have shared,
When thinking that you will this morning begin
    To be with a Whittle close *pared*.

This day you engage in a treaty, dear girl,
    No trifling, gossip or parley ;
Yet if the man's noble he'll find you a pearl,
    A wife and blessing to Charlie.

How sweet were your lips, Mary, when you
        were little,
    Your nature was gentle and fond :
Thus may they remain when you turn to a
        Whittle
    And give up your heart with a Bond.

May Charlie in *Bond*-age be joyful and *free*
    And his board supplied with good victuals ;
Long may his dear partner live happy and be
    The mother of twenty sharp Whittles.

And now from my heart may you flourish in
        peace,
    May Charles never sullenly mutter :
As seasons advance may your pleasures increase,
    Is the prayer of yours, Harry Nutter.

A SONG OF BUXTON.

TUNE—"The Rakes of Mallow."

A PROTEST ON ACCOUNT OF THE EARLY CLOSING OF THE CONCERT.

Oh ! Buxton is a pretty place,
There peace and comfort you embrace ;
A blessing to the human race
    Is health-restoring Buxton.
The limpid streams are stored with fish
That every day provide a dish,
And you may catch them when you wish,
    Then come along to Buxton.

When fever burns within your veins,
Or when by fierce rheumatic pains
Your joints are racked, what else remains
    But coming on to Buxton.
The baths will soon all pains dispel,
And make you blooming, strong and well,
Your suffering friends you then will tell
    To come along to Buxton.

You climb the hills for mountain air,
Take charming walks with ladies fair,
By night or day you'll not despair
    Upon the heights of Buxton.
In Old Poole's cavern we must own
Dame Nature's mighty works are shown,
Where stalagmites and 'tites are grown,
    Then come along to Buxton.

The Cat and Fiddle's lofty path,
The Tennis Courts and Buxton Bath
Where men are healed, if they have faith :
    Then come along to Buxton.
Good bowling greens and skating rink,
There wholesome waters you may drink,
Grand reading-rooms, for those who think,
    Are open here at Buxton.

Mysterious brigands in disguise
Will charm your ears and wondering eyes,
With wisdom, folly, truth, and lies,
    Then come along to Buxton.
But you will learn with some dismay,
The concert's o'er at close of day,
The trumpet sounds ! we slink away
    And mourn the fate of Buxton.

This brazen trumpet's piercing blast
Proclaims the entertainment's past ;
At nine o'clock ! we stand aghast
    And weep for merry Buxton.
When evening joys are incomplete
We hear the dreadful sound retreat !
Like wandering sheep we take the street,
    And ramble on in Buxton.

FINALE.

'Tis Buxton thus my pen employs,
My darling buxom girls and boys,
Through life may you all pluck some joys
    Within the vale of Buxton.
And now good-bye, God bless you all,
Success to concert, bath and ball :
I'll come to Buxton while I crawl,
    My blessings on thee, Buxton.

IN ANSWER TO SLANDEROUS WORDS

USED BY HIGGINS, THE RECORDER OF PRESTON, AND BY ADDISON, BARRISTER, AGAINST BURNLEY.

TUNE—Ash Grove.

Light hearts have good reason
For joy in each season,
When free from all treason
    They revel in bliss :
At this our grand meeting
Each other still greeting,
This year that is fleeting
    We gladly dismiss,

Our soldiers are bounding,
The Afghans surrounding,
With bugle's truce sounding
 We'll welcome them home ;
Cetewayo was haughty,
The Ameer was naughty,
Our soldiers are doughty
 Wherever they roam.

No more Isandulas,
We've conquered the Zulus,
There's scarcely a screw loose
 Throughout our domain :
The good time is coming,
Sweet peace is now blooming
With olive branch pluming,
 And long may she reign.

But let us be humble,
Or Higgins will grumble,
And Addison crumble
 Old Burnley to dust ;
Their wigs suit them quaintly,
Their gowns make them saintly,
Their words pierce but faintly,
 Because they're unjust.

This point they may rest on,
A fact we'll contest on,
We're better than Preston,
 The proud and demure ;
Our youths are as sprightly,
Our girls trip as lightly,
And smile as politely,
 With morals more pure.

Our School Board and teachers,
Our orthodox preachers
Will scorn these impeachers
    Of legal renown ;
Then ring out St. Peter
Thy bells in sweet metre,
No music is sweeter
    In proud Preston town.

Though justices slander,
And barristers pander,
They never can brand her
    With falsehood and shame ;
With her reputation
In this mighty nation,
This foul accusation
    Won't sully her name.

Though Higgins looks sternly,
And proudly may spurn thee,
We love thee old Burnley
    For deeds thou hast done ;
Let lawyers abuse thee,
With outrage accuse thee,
Yet honour imbues thee,
    Thou pride of the Brun.

THE FALL OF ALEXANDRIA.

TUNE—Bow, Wow, Wow.

The British fleet on July tenth in eighteen
    eighty two, sir,
Proclaimed to Egypt and the world, the
    wonders it could do, sir,

The Frenchman would no risk involve, but
      coolly turned away, boys,
And steered along, with high resolve, to fight
      another day, boys.
      With a cheer, boys, cheer,
Give our jolly sailor boys a cheer, boys, cheer.

The proud ambitious Arabi a rebel force united,
Ignored all friendly overtures, our power and
      honour slighted ;
Our brave commander duly gave the rebel
      leader warning,
Then opened fire from off the wave at seven in
      the morning.
      With a cheer, boys, cheer, etc.

The noble ships Penelope, Superb, and
      Temeraire,
Were handled well by men whose aim and
      courage never vary,
The Sultan and Invincible, Alexandra and the
      Condor,
The Monarch and Inflexible were belching out
      their thunder.
      With a cheer, boys, cheer, etc.

The smaller craft were manned by tars whose
      pluck was never shaken,
The Cygnet and the swift Decoy, the Bittern
      and the Beacon,
These gallant gunboats fired away, the Moslem
      forts defying,
And shared the honours of the day, with British
      colours flying.
      With a cheer, boys, cheer.

The cannon shot like lightning flew, at each
    well guarded station,
The shells fell thick within the walls with
    fearful devastation,
Egyptians and the turban'd Turk found British
    fire unpleasant,
And cursed our wicked sailors' work, when
    trampling on the crescent.
        Still a cheer, boys, cheer, etc.

Thus in one day, those ancient forts were
    promptly put to silence,
The battered walls were crumbled down by
    iron-plated violence,
This haughty chief was of no use against our
    mighty power,
He raised a lying flag of truce, and fled to Kafr
    Dowar.
        With a cheer, boys, cheer, etc.

Then let us toast our valiant tars, and their
    commander, Seymour,
Who gave the first important blow to that
    usurping dreamer,
Our soldiers bold, and Wolsley brave, for their
    decisive labour ;
And peace to those who found a grave within
    old Tel-el-Kebir.
        With a cheer, boys, cheer, etc.

And now ye anxious cotton lords, good times
    are just beginning,
May profits large attend you all in weaving and
    in spinning ;

To let you have the lion's share may merchants
    all be willing,
And on a common sixteen square your profit be
    a shilling.
      With a cheer, boys, cheer, etc.

Again adieu, my learned friends, may all our
    ways be mended,
Another fifty years, alas ! will see our lives all
    ended ;
You drank to tars, who will defend your homes
    and constitution,
And in their names I here commend this
    glorious Institution.
      With a cheer, boys, cheer, etc.

HEALEY HEIGHT.

TUNE—Jenny Jones.

One morning I strayed on the heights of old
    Healey,
Where lovers and song birds in harmony meet,
The skylark above me was chanting so freely,
The voice of the blackbird was mellow and sweet;
The throstle's song filled all the valley before me,
The robin poured out his fine song in mine ear ;
These dear, charming warblers appeared to
    adore thee,
Oh, balm-breathing Healey, sweet Healey so
    clear.

The bells of St. Peter's were ringing so sweetly,
Each heart beat on Healey with rapturous glow,
And Burnley's fair damsels were tripping so
    neatly
On the hill where the daisies and buttercups
    grow.

They may tell of Olympus, the Alps and
    Parnassus,
And snow-covered peaks far away in the west,
But the mountain I sing of is one that surpasses,
'Tis Healey, sweet Healey, the hill I love best.

'Twas here the fair daughters of Burnley stood
    gazing,
Whilst husbands and sons were engaged with
    the foe ;—
Yes, there were the matrons, with beacon fires
    blazing,
When Brunanburg's battle was raging below.
Old Venice may boast of her pleasant gondola,
And Rome may be proud of her palaces bright,
The darkie may dance in the groves of Angola,
But give me old Healey, yes, sweet Healey
    Height.

There's joy in the song of the lark, as he rises,
There's joy for his mate, as she bathes in the
    dew ;
There's joy for the boy, with the girl that he
    prizes,
There's joy in sweet friendship, that ever proves
    true.
Then sing, ye fair maids in the valley before us,
And shout, ye brave boys, your loud songs in
    the gale ;
Ye sweet, feathered songsters, still join in the
    chorus,
And chime, ye delightful old bells, through the
    vale.

THE GIRL IN THE CALICO DRESS.

TUNE—Paddle your own Canoe.

In flowery July upon Healey's proud Height,
　As the plover sprung from the morass,
And southward the cuckoo was taking his flight,
　And the corncrake was deep in the grass;
The swallow and swift were aloft in the air,
　And the starling was feeding her young;
The milkmaid was tending her cattle with care,
　And the haymakers cheerfully sung—

" The maidens of Burnley in satin or silk,
　Are pretty, I freely confess;
But give me the maid who is neatly arrayed
　In a beautiful calico dress."

They may praise the Italian ladies, in vain,
　Or the maidens of France or Peru,
Or worship the languishing beauties of Spain,
　And the blushing Circassians, too.
But she whom I love has an eye like the sloe,
　And her cheeks are like roses in June,
So graceful each step as she trips like the doe,
　And her sweet ruby lips are in tune.
　　　　　　The maidens of Burnley, &c.

Her dress (though of print) was embroidered
　　with care,
　And the flowers on her bosom were sweet;
The zephyrs waved gently her dark curly hair,
　And the buttercups bloomed at her feet.
As dew from the daisies she carelessly dashed,
　The young men were all seized with surprise;
How sweetly she smiled, and what mischief she
　　flashed
　From the glance of her dark rolling eyes.
　　　　　　The maidens of Burnley, &c.

Should fortune or friendship impel me to roam,
  Or a thirst after changes constrain,
I'd still call the banks of Old Healey my home,
  And I'd sing of its beauties again.
Sweet gardens of roses, or art-cultured bowers,
  May delight a poor soul to possess ;
But give me old Healey, bedecked with wild
    flowers,
  And the girl in the calico dress.
            The maidens of Burnley, &c.

'OLD JIM,' THE ENGINEER.

TUNE—Old Towler.

We boast of British heroes brave,
  Our valiant sons of Mars,
Are proud to see the banners wave
  Above our gallant tars.
Our bonny barks that plough the main,
  We welcome with a cheer,
But seldom sing of a railway train,
  Or a worthy engineer.
    With a hey ho chivey,
    Hark forward, hark forward tantivy.
    Then here's to Jim, make way for him !
    And keep the main line clear !

Then let my song your hearts inspire
  To trust and honour him,
That good old man we all admire,
  They call him railway Jim ;
He bids the stoker mind the brake,
  Then with his whistle clear
He makes the sleepy pointsman quake,
  Old Jim the engineer.
    With a hey ho chivey, &c.

When storms and tempests wildly rage,
　And lightnings rend the sky,
The lever doth his hands engage,
　Though thunders roll on high.
Midst danger signals, green or red,
　In fogs or darkness drear,
There's one with caution looks a-head,
　'Tis Jim the engineer.
　　With a hey ho chivey, &c.

When special trains the line invade
　Down Portsmouth's lovely dale,
Or shunted goods the rails blockade,
　Or summer trips prevail,
With watchful eye he scans the road,
　When perils dire appear,
He ne'er forgets his precious load,
　Old Jim the engineer,
　　With a hey ho chivey, &c.

On pastures green the lowing herds
　Lie fearless on the grass,
Among the woods the bonny birds
　Are chanting as we pass.
Holme's sweet sequestered glades rejoice,
　The hills, both far and near,
Re-echo loud thy engine's voice,
　Old Jim, the engineer !
　　With a hey ho chivey, &c.

In winter's cold, or summer's heat,
　I sit at ease with thee,
Mazeppa's* throbbing voice is sweet,
　'Tis always dear to me.

---

* Name of the engine.

I've not the slightest dread, indeed
    With thee I've nought to fear.
Then welcome to thy puffing steed,
    Old Jim, the engineer.
    With a hey ho chivey, &c.

OLD JIM, THE ENGINE-DRIVER.

Tune—"Poor Mary Ann."

Death throws gloom o'er every station,
                Poor old Jim!
Lower your flags—Oh, sad occasion!
                Poor old Jim!
Duty's post he well attended,
Guard and stoker oft befriended,
Now his final trip is ended,
                Poor old Jim!

Drape each signal post and depôt
                For old Jim!
Clothe in weeds his swift "Mazeppa"
                For old Jim!
Safe in charge of thy commanding,
Often have we seen thee landing,
Firmly on the engine standing,
                Brave old Jim!

Dear old Redford, all who knew thee
                Loved old Jim!
When in retrospect we view thee,
                Dear old Jim,
Memory often will remind us
Of thy honesty and kindness,
When in safety thou consigned us,
                Dear old Jim.

Through the Calder's sylvan valley,
Dear old Jim

Will " Vesuvius " no more sally
With old Jim ?

Unprotected, onward steering,
In thy dangerous charioteering,
Through the darksome tunnel peering,
Dear old Jim.

Careful by the signal steaming,
Dear old Jim ;

Still alert, with whistle screaming,
Cautious Jim :

Storms and tempests he confronted,
Always at his post when wanted,
Now, alas, old Death has shunted
Dear old Jim !

Though in sadness we bewail thee,
Dear old Jim,

Bitter storms no more assail thee,
Dear old Jim,

Angel trains express are speeding,
Heavenward pointing signals reading,
Danger lamps are fast receding,
Glorious Jim !

THE TRAM.

SUNG AT THE LITERARY AND SCIENTIFIC SOIREE, DECEMBER 13TH, 1881.

TUNE—Tramp, tramp.

Come around, my merry boys, you that merit
    earthly joys,
While I sing a simple ditty here to-night ;
Of the railway and the 'bus, people make a
    mighty fuss,
But a ride upon the tram is my delight.

CHORUS.

Then, tram, tram, tram it along the road, boys,
  With freedom, ease, and elegance combined,
You will never have a jar, as you ride upon
      the car,
  And you'll leave the rumbling omnibus
      behind.

The genius of our race has been moving on
      apace,
  And inventing everything that we require,
You can travel now with ease on to Padiham
      when you please,
  And the guard will put you down when you
      desire.
        Chorus—Tram, tram, &c.

Passing on to Brierfield, what a pleasure it will
      yield,
  When you gaze on Pendle's noble crest of
      blue :
And the silent wheels will spin, straight away
      to Nelson Inn,
  With the town of bonny Colne within the
      view.
        Chorus—Tram, tram, &c.

When conditions will afford you may trip to
      Barrowford,
  'Tis the boast of Pendle Forest, and its pride :
The sweet village in the dale, where the pretty
      girls prevail,
  Though the stately buildings stand upon one
      side.
        Chorus—Tram, tram, &c.

As you fleetly pass along, you may hear the
　　Cuckoo's song,
　And the little birds will chant upon the trees ;
You'll repose in graceful style sat upon the
　　velvet pile,
　And from danger well protected, and at ease.

Chorus—Tram, tram, &c.

There is nothing that will mar people's comfort
　　in the car,
　'Tis a place where use and ornament combine ;
Thus a lady or a queen may be proud of this
　　machine,
　As she smoothly skims away upon the line.

Chorus—Tram, tram, &c.

As along the road you pass, there will only be
　　one class,
　Where the rich and poor together may rejoice ;
There is no distinction there for an Alderman
　　or Mayor,　　　　·
　But the ladies though must always have a
　　choice.

Chorus—Tram, tram, &c.

Horses, waggonettes, and sheep, must a proper
　　distance keep,
　And the cabman with his precious little load ;
And the bridegroom with his bride must keep
　　on the proper side,
　For the tram has got a charter on the road.

Chorus—Tram, tram, &c.

You will never hear the crash of the driver's
    cruel lash,
  Nor his curses at the humble plodding team ;
But with pleasure you'll proceed by a bonny
    iron steed,
  For the easy cushioned carriage goes by
    steam.
        Chorus—Tram, tram, &c.

All the novelties in dress will around you gently
    press,
  When you take up your position in the car :
Thus you'll have a pleasant ride with a lady by
    your side,
  But the swell must go aloft with his cigar.
        Chorus—Tram, tram, &c.

A BURLESQUE

On the Reservoir Levels, Rainfalls,
Filiter's Waterworks Scheme of Robin
Hood ; and in Answer to a Correspon-
dent in the 'Gazette' signing Himself
'Good Health.'

Scene : Swindon Bank.

Good Health
(Addressing the Water Spirits) :

Why all this useless squander, tell me why ?—
Why all this lavish waste ? Ye shades reply.
Ye powers of necromancy it doth seem
That some mysterious demon haunts this stream,
Tell me ye magic spirits of the air,
Ye aqueous spirits listen to my prayer.

Without the aid of falling rain or snow
What is it makes these waters ebb and flow ?
Ye rippling rills, meandering down each dale,
Why do your numerous tributes not avail ?
Say why do melting snows, or hail or rain,
Or torrents pour their gushing streams in vain ?
Fleet speckled grouse, and simple moorland
    sheep,
Unearthly demons must around you creep !
Ye sheddings marshy, and your watery dens,
And cloud condensing hills and treacherous fens,
Wild howling whistlers through the furious
    storms :
Who shrinks the gathering ground, and thus
    transforms
The surface of this undulating scene ?
Disclose the mystery, spirits ! is it spleen ?
How strange ! though rains pour down on every
    hand,
We cross the lake like Israel on dry land.
When summer's heat dries up the mountain
    rills,
Good heavens ! without the rain the lake soon
    fills.
'Tis true that number one is sometimes high
When every inch of gathering ground is dry !

The spirits answered, ' List, my anxious friend,
These lakes do not upon the clouds depend
For their supply. My answer thus is clear,
Charge not the shades with your wild follies
    here.
Prohibited are we,' they all exclaim,
' To ears of flesh to indicate the name

Of him who wields these strange mysterious
    powers,
And fills the lakes without the aid of showers :
The freaks which our ethereal eyes behold
Must never unto mortal man be told ;
But hark ! what means that weird and dismal wail,
That from yon ponderous pipes our ears assail
With hollow tones. Good Health, be not deceived,
The spirits know thy talents, and are grieved
To know that thou should sanction give to
    schemes
Which squander money on these petty streams.
Come, honest man, if thou wouldst be discreet,
Cast now thy shoes from off thy weary feet :
The place whereon we stand is haunted ground,
And yonder massive pipes the truth resound.
I'll now convey thee through the mountain
    breeze,
And show thee wilder schemes by far than these.'

That moment by some mystic power they stood
Upon the dismal swamps of Robin Hood.
The Swindon vision fled, the Bouldsworth gale
Too keenly blew for spirits of the vale !
At once, the spirit of the mountain rill
Appeared with aspect wild. ' What is thy will,
Good Health, at this vast height above the sea,
What is thy mission; what dost want with me ?'
Inquired the ghost, with eye and voice austere.
' In search of crystal water, came I here,'
Good Health replied, ' Thou knows the district
    best,
Show me the waters which I now request !'

The spirit answered thus : ' Oh, never dream,
Or drink of this small semi-stagnant stream ;

But turn thy steps to purer vales below,
Where limpid waters in abundance flow.
Of schemes like these, thy noble mind divest,
And leave this mountain's wild tempestuous crest.
To this inconstant stream no longer cling,
But haste at once to jockey's gushing spring ;
There look around, and affluent streams you'll find,
And leave this cloudy wilderness behind.
There, bubbling rills burst out on every side,
Around a basin made by nature wide :
Then view the contour of the favoured land,
And mark the outlet where the bank should
          stand ;
A cape projects two-thirds across the vale,
Where water pressure never could prevail.
Old nature, with a friendly forethought keen,
From east to west has left a bank between,
Where honest men of competence and sense
Could safely seal the gap at small expense ;
But engineers, when on such schemes they're bent,
Their eye is firmly fixed on five per cent.
Look round to neighbouring boroughs I could
          name,
Whose spendthrift works are now a lasting
          shame,
Their rates are raised to prop some alien scheme,
Though local men condemned it as a dream,
A fact experience often times has shown,
That prophets in their country are not known,
The spirits see (and often are enraged)
That talent by the distance now is gauged.

To bring my friendly mission to an end,
Take this advice : upon thyself depend :
Let not professions, foreign, low or high,
Against thy common sense thy wants supply.

Though engineers draw plans and lines
        complete,
They're oft unlearned on rocks beneath their
        feet.
Then let your neighbour's wisdom, not his
        birth,
Be duly weighed, and valued at its worth ;
The city phantom, title proud and vain,
On rural wisdom looks with proud disdain,
Then mark my parting words with rigorous heed,
True worth is not in title, rank, or creed,
And now, Good Health, my honest friend adieu,'
The vision then with kindred spirits flew.

LITERARY AND SCIENTIFIC CLUB DINNER.

TUNE—" Nancy Dawson."

Ye noble men with learning fraught,
Who leading questions long have taught,
And have with superstition fought,
        In this great age of science :
Take heed my friends that sit around,
Who scientific truths expound,
Till certain data you have found
        Pray never yield compliance.

This night we set apart for glee,
At this our special jubilee,
We spend the time in harmony,
        As happy mortals can do.
No question we to-night discuss,
So I will rhyme our syllabus,
This club is now unanimous—
        This science propaganda,

Our officers are most discreet,
With fifteen members now complete ;
The president gets on his feet
    As Henry Houlding rises.
Friends Brumwell, Grant and Anningson,
J. Langfield Ward, A. Waddington,
And Mr. Strange is also one
    Of our notorious vices.

Our grand committee's names you want,
Whose hearts for useful knowledge pant ;
The first I name is Lewis Grant,
    Who able service lends you.
J. Monkman, Lancaster, F. Hill,
B. Sagar, Roberts,—men of skill,
And two that useful places fill,
    J. Kay and J. Mackenzie.

The opening paper of the year
Was read by one who made it clear,
That England was the pioneer
    Of honest legislation.
By fact and figure he impressed,
(And proved by many a searching test),
That Britain had far more progressed
    Than any other nation.

Not more than forty years ago,
When food was high, and wages low,
Before the corn bill's overthrow
    The taxes were oppressing.
Sir Ughtred J. Kay-Shuttleworth
Said, England had been stepping forth
Among the nations of the earth,
    In peace and wealth progressing.

The second paper critics say,
Was written well by William Kay,
On southern California,
    The golden land he went to.
With humming birds and turtle doves,
Fleet antelopes, the huntsman loves ;
The towering pines, and orange groves
    Of glorious Sacramenta.

Of Cashmere Vale in Industan,
Where dwells the proud Mohammedan,
Friend Doxy brought a map or plan
    Of all the peninsula.
There tall Himalayan cedars grow,
In Chuna bowers the roses blow,
Where Juilam's river rushes through
    The pass of Baramula.

We shall a pleasant story hear
Of Cecil Slingsby's short career,
Among the wolves and Norway deer,
    On Galdhoppigen's mountain.
The snow-capped peak, the swampy fen,
The Salten river, and Ramsen,
The Sauren, Drammen, and Glommen,
    And Tanar's lonely fountain.

Upon the wretched cotton trade
Friend Greenwood next will make a raid,
He'll show how profits may be made
    By proper calculation—
Statistics too from first to last,
Both of the present and the past,
And of the future, a forecast,
    Without exaggeration.

Then Doctor Monkman will dispel
All former doubts, and wonders tell
Of ages past, and what befel
    At certain times and stages.
He'll speak of icebergs long ago,
And mighty slips of mountain snow,
Where land was raised or sunk below
    In prehistoric ages.

We know Frank Nicholson has toiled,
And many a useful hour beguiled;
With animals which now run wild;
    He knows each name and habit
The British weasel, mouse and rat,
The fox, the hedgehog and pole-cat,
The squirrel, deer, the mole and bat,
    The otter, hare and rabbit.

J. Grant is the interpreter,
Of a lithographic soiree, sir,
From stone to paper he'll transfer
    A well defined impression,
The printing process upon stone
Which has to such perfection grown,
Will then by him be clearly shown
    In certain quick succession.

The meeting next, J. Langfield Ward
(For whom this Club has great regard)
Will name the Frogs of a Grecian bard,
    Their greatest comic writer,
Who wrote some brilliant comedies,
And ridiculed wise Socrates;
Than this great Aristophanes
    Few poets have been brighter.

The ensuing evening, Mr. Finn
With modern epic will begin,
And doubtless will the favour win
    Of this grand institution.
I now must try to expedite,
Lest I should mar your appetite,
For I appear the following night,
    Discussing evolution.

The annual meeting comes the next,
When our officials get perplexed,
While some have reason to be vexed,
    And others will be merry ;
Then many evenings stand between
Before a meeting we convene.
Let Mr. Midgely close the scene
    With a good dramatic soiree.

ON THE REMOVAL OF THE MAYOR'S LAMPS.

Ye neighbours, come join my affliction and
        sorrow,
    Our darkness and gloom have begun ;
From your vision the lamps will be taken to-
        morrow,
    And raised near the banks of the Brun !
From the dusk to the dawn they will never
        more light us,
    No longer protect us from scamps ;
For the loss of their splendour there's nought
        to requite us,
    Oh ! what shall we do without lamps.

Our borough's chief magistrate, shield and
    defender,
  Two years having faithfully reigned ;
Will cheerfully doff, and on Wednesday tender,
  The cloak and regalia unstained.
At the court he will gracefully bow to the
    bench,
  On the day when his worship decamps :
Then he'll lecture the council and bid them
    retrench,
  When taking his leave of the lamps.

When the chair is adorned by his prudent
    successor,
  With aldermen smiling around ;
Of goodness and mercy may he be possessor,
  With wisdom and judgment profound.
When an alderman's horn is well-budded and
    pointed,
  He merits the seals and the stamps ;
With the oil of the morning then have him
    anointed,
  And give him a couple of lamps.

The children of Israel, when homeward
    returning,
  Well pleased with an enemy's spoil,
Would order a number of lamps to be burning,
  And fully provided with oil.
'Neath the pillar or cloud, famous Aaron and
    Moses
  Securely reclined in their camps ;
Thus a mayor on his couch as securely reposes,
  When duly protected with lamps.

A lamp for a mayor in whom we can trust is
    An emblem of honour, a mark
And a light to the feet in the path of a justice,
    Like Bezaleel's glorious ark.
The lamp of the wicked will flicker and perish,
    Wherever on earth he encamps ;
But the glory and strength of the righteous
        shall flourish,
    When properly lighted with lamps.

A BRAVE TOWNSMAN.

Read on the occasion of Thomas Dewhurst receiving
a purse of gold for rescuing from drowning seven
lives.

When nations to war's wicked influence yield,
    And feelings revengeful create,
When armies are sweeping the forest and field,
    To plunder a neighbouring State,
The angel of darkness, with terrible swoop,
    Brings ruin commercial, and death,
The vine and the olive trees sicken and droop,
    With a touch of its poisonous breath.

When war's mighty engines, with shivering
        boom,
    Strike kingdoms with dreadful alarms,
How little we think, till our dear happy home
    Is robbed of its circle of charms,
The army and navy, when evil portends,
    Are pillars on which we rely,
Defending our country, our homes and our
        friends,
    More dauntless when danger is nigh.

The tears and the thanks of Great Britain are due,
 And tendered with grateful regard,
To the lions whose standard is red, white and
     blue,
 And these are a nation's award.
In guarding our country, to die with the brave,
 Is ranked among glorious deeds,
Yet 'tis nobler to rescue from danger, and save
 The son of a widow in weeds.

Brave men we have yet who imperil their lives,
 The one whom this evening we toast,
Is dauntless in danger, and manfully strives
 Not to kill, but to save is his boast.
May his heart never fail nor his courage decline
 When perils in future may come,
But like a true hero with pleasure consign
 The drowning boys safe to their home.

When his ears are assailed by a shriek of
     distress,
 To assist like an arrow he flies;
His arms are extended to rescue and bless,
 Regardless of pension or prize.
For many long years, may the lives he has
     saved
 Do honour to Dewhurst's good name;
And at last o'er his dust let the facts be
     engraved,
 Recording the deeds of his fame.

ON THE BIRTHDAY OF A NIECE.

Many happy returns of the day
 I now wish you, and bless you, dear niece,
And as seasons keep rolling away,
 May your wisdom and pleasures increase.

On this earth, with its troubles and strife,
    May you never in vain seek a friend,
But in comfort and peace throughout life,
    Be a blessing, and blessed to the end.

May your heart remain kindly and warm,
    And your mind be a fountain of bliss ;
May your life to your friends be a charm,
    And your temper no worse than it is.

THE MAYOR OF BRUNSWICK.

Ye fountains bursting from the rock or fen,
That sweetly flow through Ormerod's lovely
    glen,
From Holme's laburnum groves, or Derply's
    crown,
In limpid streams to serve our ancient town ;
Just when your wandering, useful waters meet
In foaming torrents wild, each other greet,
Then clap your hands, ye floods, with joy
    declare
That Brunswick sacred temple owns a mayor.

Ye holy steeples pointing to the sky,
Unfurl your banners only half mast high ;
Let Wesleyans weep with unavailing tears,
Their prestige now is gone for two long years,
And mourn ye proud deserted banks of Brun,
Your sister Calder doth exulting run
Beside the stately church and civic chair,
Where worships Brunswick's modest, gracious
    mayor.

Flow on, sweet Calder, through the wide domain,
By Towneley's ancient hall and sacred fane,
Roll down, ye mountain streams, in surging pride,
When nearing Brunswick pray more gently glide,
Rush as ye will in rough tempestuous style,
But smoothly skim when near the noble pile :
Let storms and tempests, floods and lightnings
      spare
The glorious temple, and its honoured mayor.

Ye lofty chimneys, black with poisonous smoke,
By rods protected from the lightning's stroke,
Pour out your breath, and nod each sooty crest ;
Tell hungry sea-gulls rambling from the west
In search of distant coasts, and calmer seas—
To waft the tidings by each passing breeze—
And every wild bird floating through the air
Proclaim the joyful news of Brunswick's mayor.

Ye prudent councillors will honour gain
By circling Brunswick's son with civic chain :
Pay due regard, and strict obedience show ;
He can suspend, or can enforce the law.
Ye portly aldermen, ye honoured few,
Give veneration when 'tis fairly due ;
Ye learned clerks that sit around, beware ;
And duly reverence Brunswick's noble mayor.

Sing out, sweet choir, and spread the glorious
      news,
Thou sacred pulpit, and ye spacious pews
Re-echo from the gilded pillars round,
To join the diapason's deepest sound ;
Let teachers, scholars, too, the theme prolong,
And all the congregation join in song ;
Thus with united breath and fervent prayer
Bring blessings rich upon our Brunswick mayor.

With trembling pen I humbly dare to trench
Upon the sacred threshold of the bench,
Where sits impartial justice on her throne,
And villains cringe with penitential groan.
May justice guard the pure and good from ill,
And seize the guilty with unerring skill ;
Let nine escape, yea rather nineteen Cains,
Than let one guiltless Abel die in chains ;
If honest doubt distract one troubled breast,
Release the wretch, your honours, 'tis the best,
The grapes of Eshcol then shall crown the fare
Of   Burnley's   magistrates, and   Brunswick's
          mayor.

A BIRTHDAY RHYME.

The earth's daily motion brings darkness and
          light,
The light is called day, and the darkness is
          night ;
Three hundred and sixty-five days and six
          hours,
Give a year's busy changes, through sunshine
          and showers.
We speed round the sun as he shines in the sky,
A thousand long miles in a minute we fly.
The planets' centripetal circuit will bring
The summer and autumn, the winter and spring.
As it swiftly moves through the celestial signs,
Three-and-twenty degrees and a half it inclines
To the plane of its orbit, and this I suppose
Brings the change of the seasons ; a natural
          cause.

So long as the axis inclines, never mourn,
The seed time and harvest will surely return ;
Each year into seasons this angle divides ;
The moon's great attraction produces the tides.
While great revolutions keep sweeping along,
We'll honour our friends in a cup or a song,
Our wives and our sweethearts, we love and
        embrace,
While millions of worlds are revolving in space.
And thus, as this earth in its whirligig course,
Is held by the sun's gravitation and force,
So is he who is married and settled in life,
Compelled by a power to revolve round his wife.
She brightens his home with caresses and smiles,
Whate'er be his conduct, she seldom reviles.
And now, my dear lady, I honestly pray,
That you may see many returns of the day.
When riper in years, may you never despair,
Though children's dear children encircle your
        chair ;
And their little branches I hope you will see,
To honour the stem of the darling old tree.
'Tis a wish, yea a prayer ! that I fervently utter,
As witness the signature, friend Harry Nutter.

SONG.

*Written on the occasion of a visit of ten members
of the Burnley Literary and Scientific Club to
Lothersdale.*

TUNE—'Cork Leg.'

Ye prudent and wise who are not very grave,
Whose earnest attention I fervently crave,
I know that you honour the witty and brave
Who went on a visit to Lothersdale cave,
        Ri too ral loo, &c.

These ten merry boys, during holiday time,
Once entered a cavern deep down in the lime,
If you'll join in the chorus, a musical chime,
I'll give you their names mingled up in my
    rhyme,
      Ri too ral loo, &c.

Although our director had learning and skill,
We had plenty of fun when ascending the *Hill*,
His scholars were sportive and would not be
    still,
Yet while he was *Witham* he got his own *Will*,
      Ri too ral loo, &c.

You will *Grant* that this question required a
    wide range,
When the mountains before us were subject to
    change,
On the south of the valley near Lothersdale
    grange,
Where the rocks are upheaved and appear
    rather *Strange*,
      Ri too ral loo, &c.

Wild animals roamed in this beautiful dell,
At a time so remote that no mortal can tell,
They ranged through this county and Yorkshire
    as well,
From *Lancaster* castle to *Waddington* fell,
      Ri too ral loo, &c.

We could not old Whalley or Clitheroe see,
Nor the castle or sacred monastery
Where the *Ward* and the *Monkman* used to be—
'Twas a *Nutter* impossibility,
      Ri too ral loo, &c.

ON THE OCCASION OF MISS HORNER LEAVING BURNLEY

For the Royal Academy of Music, Jan. 1st, 1888.

A maiden's song we often heard,
  In charming numbers spun ;
But now the dear harmonious bird
  Has fled the banks of Brun.

Through Calder's vale, each fragrant bower,
  And rippling burn and spring
Will murmur sadly, till the hour
  She homeward spreads her wing.

A temper kind, a graceful frame,
  Retiring and discreet ;
Her voice, a kindling mellow flame,
  Than Miriam's voice more sweet.

Our Choral Unions sadly moan,
  Her loss they deeply feel ;
And local bards in fervent tone,
  Petition for her weal.

May health her tuneful voice sustain
  Throughout the passing year ;
When merry Christmas comes again,
  We'll give her welcome cheer.

The organ's diapason deep,
  Its solemn tones shall lend ;
The fiddle with its glorious cheep,
  Shall her sweet voice attend.

Messiah's songs, and sweet refrains,
  She'll render true and clear ;
And in Creation's noblest strains,
  Will charm the finest ear.

May honest friends and future fame
Give joy in years to come ;
And merit give an honoured name
To bless her home, sweet home.

ON THE PRESENTATION TO
MR. LEWIS GRANT

*For Services rendered to the Burnley Literary
and Scientific Club.*

When told that a gift was in store for our
    friend,
The Muses I summoned at once to attend ;
Those Queens of Parnassus are artful and shy,
Too modest at times or o'er proud to reply.
Could dew from the wings of one goddess
    descend,
And moisten my quill till a poem I'd penned—
Or give it a dip in the helicon stream,
Oh ! then would each stanza adorn this high
    theme.
I've hailed the sweet Muses since I was a boy,
And found them unwilling, conceited, and coy,
Their favours poetic, still distant I scan,
I rhyme on without them as well as I can.
Regardless of measure I scribble each line,
Deserted or shunned by the musical nine,
But if I this evening Parnassus could clime
I'd stamp Lewis Grant on the sands of old time.
This night we convene, and each member is
    proud
To gratefully thank him for labours bestowed.
This purse, and address where our mites have
    been cast,
Are trifles compared to his work of the past.

These tokens of honour, of love, and respect
For toils volunteered, with such valid effect,
Are tendered with grateful and fervent regard,
And so are the lines of your servant the bard.
With kindness of heart for this club he has
    striven,
So also our hearts have responsively given,
No timepeice of marble, Sicilian cold,
But nuggets of ophar, or Balarat gold.
The dear, precious metal is sometimes a curse,
Yet Shakespeare advises, get gold in thy purse.
We honour friend Grant for his heart and his
    head,
For man is the goud, honest Robin hath said.

That Lewis may live a long life and be blessed,
Is a wish that's re-echoed from every breast,
No discord in life his enjoyments should mar,
His years should make infants of Jenkins and
    Parr.

For all our excursions he marked out a plan,
With kindness he catered and led up the van,
Through sacred cathedrals with reverence he
    steered—
And abbeys in ruins most dismal and weird;
Where poets and painters once flourished and
    died,
Friend Lewis was chosen commander and guide;
Could we have our wishes his name and his home
Should have a grand record for ages to come.
The sights we have witnessed by mountain and
    dale,
Are more than my muse can with prudence
    detail.

Through manors and castles with ample
      demesnes,
Where oft were imprisoned proud England's
      good queens.
Through colleges also with high nodding towers,
With telescopes mounted, of marvellous powers,
By their aid Father Perry can nightly descry
Ten millions of suns in the depths of the sky.
Churches we entered and filed down the naves ;
Stained windows we gazed at with grand
      architraves.
And now Mr. Lewis I'll bid you adieu,
Your labours now passed we are pleased to
      review.
Your modest successor now fills up the void,
Like yourself he's good natured, kind, *una*-Lloyd
He will stick to his post for this reason, I say
You have left him in charge of a *Ward* and a
      †Kay.

JOB WHITTAM HARTLEY, GUARDIAN.

A MEMENTO.

The poor man's friend, the pauper's stay,
No more his genial smiles will play,
With doubtful glance, or humour gay,
        At morn or noon :
Job's useful life has passed away,
        Alas ! too soon.

---

*President,   †Treasurer,

Ye kind protectors of the poor,
The friend you've met so oft before,
His welcome face you'll see no more !—
        Ye guardian class—
The threshold of the council door
        No more he'll pass !

The workhouse ! misery's last retreat,
No more resounds his well-known feet !
The wretched there no more will greet
        Their generous friend :
No more his kindly heart will beat,
        Nor hand extend.

Ye outdoor poor, in pain and grief,
Who weekly cringe to claim relief !
In dust now lies your guardian chief,
        In his last robe :
Grim death has nipt the yellow leaf
        Of honest Job !

Ye frugal poor, of lean estate,
Who duly pay your yearly rate,
And struggle with an adverse fate—
        The brave unknown—
You've lost a friend and advocate,
        In him that's gone !

And you that deal with cautious hand
The hard earned rates, don't reprimand
The worthy poor, that starving band,
        Nor curse and rave ;
Your child or sister so may stand,
        And humbly crave !

TO MISS NANNIE MAY C——.

Your appearance on earth was a blessing divine,
In the year eighteen hundred and sixty and
   nine ;
You were born in December, the seventeenth
   day,
Yet your name like your nature, dear Nannie,
   is May.
As your life is unfolding discretion acquire,
Let your conduct be such as your parent's
   desire,
Study closely old nature, her laws to explore,
Learning something each day that you knew
   not before.
Be established in truth ; be brave, but not rude ;
And more anxious to listen than rashly obtrude ;
Trusted secrets disclose not ; be true to your
   friends ;
If you thoughtlessly vex, pray, at once make
   amends.

For all favours be grateful, but fawning despise.
Silly gossips avoid, pay regard to the wise ;
To the pauper be kind, though he oftentimes
   pleads,
For this life's highest pleasures are generous
   deeds ;
Violent passions restrain, never envy nor sneer,
Make a name to be loved by a noble career.
And now, in conclusion, my dear Nannie May,
I hope you'll have many returns of the day ;
From childhood I've loved you, before you
   could utter
The name of your friend and subscriber,
   H. Nutter.

FLOWERS FROM THE TOMBS OF THE BARDS.

Written in answer to a letter containing flowers gathered near the graves of Shelley and Keats, by a friend, and sent from Rome.

Many thanks for your letter and kindly regards,
And the flowers that you culled from the tombs
     of the bards.
Sweet emblems of love from the sacred retreats,
Where repose the dear ashes of Shelley and
     Keats.
Though a joy to me, yet, not for ever, I fear,
For the violet's soft petals are now turning sear,
I shall keep and protect them in crystalline urns,
And adorn them with leaves from the shrine of
     Rob Burns,
There to rest till their delicate fibres decay,
And by slow dissolution have fallen away,
Then the dust I will cherish, protect, and retain,
While the visible atoms of matter remain,
As they mingle and change undisturbed on the
     shelf,
From the rude hand of danger I'll shield them
     myself,
Till the last debt to nature I finally pay—
And thus like the leaves and the flowers, drop
     away.

TO MISS F. E. J., ON HER TWENTY-FIRST BIRTHDAY.

Dear Florence, this day is the last in the year
    That numbers you twenty-and-one ;
Henceforth you may boast of a woman's career,
    Until the last circuit is run.

Seven thousand six hundred and seventy days
  Have passed since the hour of your birth,
And through the whole number your genial ways
  Have made you a blessing on earth.

Your heart is not poisoned with envy or pride,
  But heaves with compassionate swell ;
Your future in life, if the past be a guide,
  Will prove that dame Eve never fell.

Now life's verdant season with you is in bloom ;
  May summer your pleasures increase ;
May autumn be free from all sorrow and gloom ;
  And then may your winter be peace.

And now Florence Ellen, I fervently pray
  That your heart may keep happy and true ;
A hundred returns of your dear natal day
  I now wish you.   Dear lady adieu.

A STORY OF A POODLE.

My dear Mister Editor Houlding,
  With poets I never was classed ;
I neither want praising nor scolding,
  For either the present or past.

But I ask to relate you a story,
  In plain honest doggerel verse ;
Though clear as the waters of Shorey,
  The spring is undoubtedly worse.

A man of a generous nature,
  Though not over foolish or wise,
Will love a kind innocent creature,
  And not o'er a brute tyrannise.

Their use and devotion compel us
    To love them and even caress ;
Yet cruel cantankerous fellows
    Will torture the things they possess.

I once had a bonny French poodle,
    A cunning affectionate thing,
At my feet she would fondle and cuddle,
    But she strayed one morning in spring.

She deserted the home she was born in,
    The cottage wherein she was reared ;
In your paper on Saturday morning,
    This curious notice appeared :

" Lost, stolen, or strayed, I cannot tell which,
A beautiful dark faced poodle bitch,
With dark brown eyes, and an excellent smell,
Her ears are uncut, and she answers to Nell.
Her action is good, though her tail is unfurled,
She's a regular swell as she trots through the
       world,
A handsome reward any person will get,
Who brings to my office that brute of a pet."

On the morrow she came with a caper,
    I know not how she was constrained ;
But she followed the boy with your paper,
    As if she knew what it contained.

I had scarcely unfastened the shutter,
    The boy had just opened the door ;
'Tis as true as my name's Harry Nutter,
    That Nellie jumped on to the floor.

A POEM IN SCOTCH.

The following poem is dedicated to a Scotch friend,
Dr. Mackenzie, the honorary secretary to the
Burnley Literary and Scientific Club.

Dear doctor, ye should na be stealin awa,
Ayont the north border by clachan and ha ;
Owre braid rairing rivers whare warriors hae
      baithed,
Whare foes ha been dunted and friends muckle
      scaithed.

Ye braw winsome swankie, ye're in your hot
      bluid,
I thought ye were willyart, auldfarren an guid ;
Ye're mislear'd an sleekit, in rinning aff hame—
But aiblins wanrestful and seeking a dame.

It gars us feel lanely an maistly unweel,
To lose sik a birkie and leesome young chiel ?
And thus in your absence we canna do mair,
Than greet for a brither, till hameward ye steer.

The excursion ye planned had excited our
      hopes,
That you would gang with us to Pendle's wild
      slopes ;
Although ye were absent we gat a good drive,
An the wonders we saw there I'll try to descrive.

Auld abbeys sae eldritch are there to be found,
Whare the mavis and lintwhite sing sweetly
      around ;
The bumclock hums freely, the laverock sings
      high—
Fond cushats coo safely nae oulet is high.

Auld mansions are lonely and crumblin away,
Now feckless and worset, to time they're a prey ;
Yet ance they were poughty an weel fortified,
An swats and thick bannocks were freely supplied.

Armorial bearings were over the door,
An gurgoyles projected behind and before ;
The ghaistly old rooms were all fairly weel lit,
An cuspated winnocks were mullioned wi grit.

The ramparts are standing, wi ivy they're green,
Where Henry de Hoghton ruled over the scene ;
At Mearley brave warriors hae met wi their death,
An valiant Lord Sussex here drew his first breath.

The biggins are ouric, the chimlies are braid,
Their walls ance so stalwart are maistly decayed;
Ane's fashed and unsicker, for warlocks are there,
An bogles might scaith us when speeling the stair.

We gloured an we graipit and muckle we swat,
Our sarks amaist dripping, our breeks might be
            wat—
An doubtless our hearts were all melting like wax,
Our knees were unsicker and feckless our backs.

The lightning was flashing—we glinted wi fear,
Lest boggarts should fleg us and then disappear—
The streamlet near Mearley dashed by in a flood,
An Pendle's proud summit was cap't wi a clud.

No skelpies we saw there to scar and to fash,
Yet witches were with us, baith cannie an gash ;
Not soft menseless gaukies, nae gossip or sneak,
But sonsie young maidens, and dames unco meek.

No pibroch was sounded your friends to salute,
But through the weird mansion re-echoed the flute,
Which rallied our party in Mearley's old shrine :
We finished our labours wi singing Lang Syne.

Then backlins we hastened weel pleased wi the
        day,
Though some of our brithers had wandered away;
A guid tea was served at the Brounlaw Hotel,
Ramfeezl'd and droukit we relished it well.

GLOSSARY.

The following glossary will be found to contain
explanations of some of the terms and phrases used
in the above poem :—

HA, hall.

SCAITHED, injured.

WILLYART, bashful.

AULDFARREN, sagacious.

AIBLINS WANRESTFUL,
perhaps restless.

BIRKIE, young man.

LEESOME CHIEL, plea-
sant fellow.

MAVIS AND LINTWHITE,
thrush and linnet.

CUSHATS, stock doves.

POUGHTY, proud.

SWATTS—BANNOCKS, ale
and Scotch bread.

OURIE, drooping.

BOGLES, goblins.

SCAITH, harm.

GLOURED AN WIGRAIPIT
stared and groped

UNSICKER — FECKLESS,
unsafe—weak.

CANNIE AND GASH,
gentle and wise.

SONSIE, sweet and en-
gaging.

RAMFEEZL'D AN DROU-
KIT, fatigued and wet.

CLACHAN, village.

DUNTED, beaten.

BRAW WINSOME SWAN-
KIE, hearty young man.

MISLEAR'D AND SLEEKIT
mischievous and sly.

GARS, makes.

MAISTLY, mostly.

GREET, weep.

ELDRITCH, frightful.

BUMCLOCK, humming
beetle.

FECKLESS AND WORSET,
weak and worsted.

GHAISTLY, ghostly.

WINNOCKS, windows.

FASHED AN UNSICKER,
troubled and unsafe.

SPEELING, climbing.

SWAT, sweat.

SARKS, shirts.

WAT, wet.

FLEG, random blow.

SKELPIES, water spirits.

MENSELESS GAUKIES,
ill-mannered, half-
witted.

BACKLINS, homeward.

MUCKLE, much.

ON THE OCCASION OF THE
REV. WILLIAM REID LEAVING NELSON.

I'm sorry, dear Amos, in fact, I am grieving,
To learn that your parson is talking of leaving.
Just allow me to warn'you, in this humble letter,
'Tis a thousand to one that you'll e'er get a
    better ;
You may get a man prouder, and full of pretence,
But not like your REID, with his sound common
    sense.
He is gentle and kind—also bold and outspoken,
And no one can call him a *Reed* that is broken ;
His purpose is honest, and simple his creed,
That a fool need not err, and a runner may
    Read.
May he ne'er lack a shilling, a friend, or a
    dinner,
Is the earnest desire of a brother and sinner ;
May his years be prolonged, and may age bring
    him ease,
And his passage from life be by painless disease.
In the dark shades of death may his pillow be
    soft,
And his password be ' Jesus,' when soaring aloft ;
May angels attend the last words he can utter,
Is the prayer of his personal friend, Harry
    Nutter.

              —To Mr. Amos, secretary.

THE ROYAL VISIT TO BURNLEY.

Hail ! grandson of our noble Queen,
    And Albert Edward's son,
Our banners wave in blue and green,
    A welcome on the Brun.

This day we politics abjure,
 And with one mind evince
A welcome by the rich and poor
 To Albert Victor, Prince.

And when in distant future years
 He dons the British crown,
May he throughout both hemispheres
 Have earned a high renown.

No potency can e'er obtain,
 Or monarch long endure,
Unless the people's hearts he gain,
 His throne is insecure.

May manly deeds and noble worth
 Embellish his career,
And be to every Prince on earth
 A glorious pioneer.

THE QUEEN AND JOHN BRIGHT.

In reference to Bright's defence of Her Majesty's absence from public life after the death of Prince Albert.

I'll sing you a song of a lady ;
 The Queen of our sea-beaten isle,
This dear little creature was ready
 To welcome John Bright with a smile ;
' Your friendship I'm happy to make, sir,'
 The Queen of Great Britain began,
' Your Sovereign you'll never forsake, sir,
 But stand in defence like a man.

My daughter is waiting to greet you,
    The Princess of Prussia is here ;
She has come to old Windsor to meet you,
    For Bright is a name she holds dear ;
Long time she's been anxiously waiting,
    And casting her eye to the door,
And now she's the pleasure of meeting
    The friend of the perishing poor.

Your speeches we read with great pleasure,
    They're faithful, and loyal, and true,
Your words of affection we treasure,
    And ever feel grateful to you.'
As she gazed on the Liberal chieftain
    A tear in her eye might be seen ;
She said, ' You're the kindest of statesmen,
    You defended your widowed Queen.

I thought of your kind benediction
    When moistening my couch with a tear,
Lamenting in deepest affliction
    The loss of a partner so dear ;
When my heart was sinking in sadness,
    Your words were a source of relief ;
And now I can welcome with gladness,
    Old England's great Liberal chief.'

THE MAYOR'S DINNER.

My Dear Mr. Mayor, at your call I'll be there,
    On the thirtieth day of October ;
At the name of a dinner, like many a sinner,
    I turn up again like Micauber.

As chief magistrate I am bound to relate,
    That your conduct has always inclined
To pity and pardon. Yet those you were hard on,
    Got justice, with mercy combined.

When the ruffian or wench stood arraigned
    at the bench,
You were touched with their pitiful wailings,
But when you had chided, you sighed, and
    decided,
And thought of your own little failings.

Through each busy year I have watched your
    career,
And am proud to declare without scorn,
That the badge and the chain will be never
    again
More kindly or faithfully worn.

The brave and the witty, give judgement with
    pity,
Regardless of evil reports,
But we who are nervous, may goodness
    preserve us
From magistrates, lawyers, and courts.

IN ANSWER TO A PRESENT.

Dear Lady, the presents arrived, with your card,
For which, pray accept the best thanks of a
    bard ;
With care the dear parcel at once I unpacked,
The contents of which I began to extract :
When lo ! to my wonder and grateful surprise,
Two gray speckled water-fowl gladdened my
    eyes,
Their weight and condition I gauged by a lift,
And honoured the feelings that prompted the
    gift.

The dear little ducklings were tenderly bred,
No game could be richer, no birds better fed ;
The fowl were delicious, the best of their kind
To please a man's palate, the keen or refined.
Although they were welcome, in time, and in
    place,
It was not the beauty, or weight of the brace
That gave me the pleasure, or measured their
    worth,
Or kindled emotions my bosom heaved forth,
Though plump and well-flavoured, and tender
    each part,
Their value I prized by the donor's kind heart.
In friendship's true standard, the heart is the guide,
'Twas therefore I relished the ducklings with
    pride.
Your dutiful husband, no doubt had a voice
In point of selection ; and wise was his choice,
Not only in water-fowl, partridge, or snipe,
But judgment in game of a far nobler type,
The test of his wisdom's criterion was true,
When his heart's warm affections centred on you,
Whose bosom was faithful, untainted and fair,
'Twas then that a dear tender duckling you were.
But now to my pen a strong brake I'll apply,
To wander still further, my Muse is too shy,
Such terms of endearment as duckling, my friend,
Must bring my effusion, though short, to an end.

WRITTEN FOR THE VICTORIA ASSEMBLY ROOM, DECEMBER 31, 1887.

The year will end when you observe this night
The hands upon the dial stand upright ;
Our time is measured by this whirling sphere,
To-night at twelve she marks another year.

On this last day, just when the year is spun,
Our wicked world is nearest to the sun.
Though swift the planet round her orbit roves,
When near the sun with greater speed she
        moves.
And yet there's not the slightest jar or sound,
As this huge globe flies in her circuit round.
Bound to her path, by Sol's attractive force,
She turns upon her axis in her course.
From West to East she daily tumbles o'er,
While eight and sixty thousand miles an hour
She rolls along her wondrous yearly flight
Around the glorious central orb of light.
She lingers not when at the winning post,
But flies along the course.   She's never lost;
Swift circling round the sun in endless space,
Attended by the moon, with smiling face.
The mighty orb, of light and heat the source,
Keeps moons and planets in sweet intercourse.
The earth's diurnal movement tells the hours;
Days, weeks, and years are marked as round
        she tours.
The sage will soon depart, Old Eighty-seven,
With all the cares and pleasures he has given ;
Young Eighty-eight takes up the race again,
He must alike the usual speed maintain.
Before the earth once more flies round the sun,
May Horner find you wisdom, wit, and fun.
Our Queen the year of jubilee survives ;
No monarch in this world more truly strives
To keep a kindly sympathetic bond
With subjects here at home, and those beyond
The seas ; the millions, south, and east, and
        west,
Whom no terrestrial monarch dare molest.

No Sovereign of the past so loved has been
As our Victoria, honoured, widowed Queen.
The prayer of each one here is this, that she
May long survive her year of jubilee,
To rule in peace a people brave and free.

'Tis just four days and sixty-seven weeks,
Since we commenced our funny friendly freaks
In this grand room, wherein we meet to-night—
This hall of splendour, reared for your delight.
Already what a mighty void it fills,
What joy, and useful lessons it instils.
Our greatest poets' fancies, flights and dreams :
Their potent proverbs, and exalted themes
Are here interpreted, with instinct clear,
For your instruction, guidance, hope and cheer.
From year to year our special aim shall be
To keep the moral tone both high and free.
The villain's deep laid schemes we here expose,
When rounds of hearty, well-deserved applause
Burst from the lusty throats above, below,
At each designing rascal's overthrow.
When victory crowns a brave and noble deed,
Or loving hearts for others intercede,
When honest worth receives its just reward,
And fiends are from their deadly game debarred,
With these portrayed, when voice and act
    combine,
'Tis then the stage fulfills her high design.

We prize our high class sweet orchestral band,
Which timely answers the conductor's wand.
From cornet, fiddle, flute and clarionette,
Down to the double bass, we music get.
No selfish Calvinistic creeds we preach,
But broad and human principles we teach.

All shades of politics we here abjure,
From bribery and corruption we are pure.
From some imperial matters we dissent,
At times we blame our local parliament.
Our councillors and aldermen and mayors
Have had a large amount of local cares ;
Our new fledged mayor we wish him health and
       peace,
May all that's good surround him and increase,
And when he justice metes to hardened sinners,
May he be merciful to young beginners.

When we compare with boroughs here around,
Our rates are less than theirs, sir, in the pound ;
Although our gas is cheap and shineth clear,
It yields a golden harvest year by year ;
Our streets, hotels, and shops are bright and
       gay,
With nineteen candle gas of lustrous ray,
Trees, hills and clouds are shining as we pass,
The heavens declare the power of Burnley gas.
That this department pays, you clearly see,
And blazes brightly 'neath the *Greenwood* tree.

From gas to water : Now we come in view
Of mountains, where the moorcock and curlew
Skim o'er the cloud-capt, rugged summit, free ;
And mountain lambs are sheltering on the lee,
Those distant, filtering hills of millstone grit,
By Vulcan's power upheaved, or lightning split,
Where rocky glens and heath-clad vales abound,
And ancient, prehistoric urns are found.

Brave Wilkinson ! we thank thee now at last,
For glimpses thou hast furnished of the past ;
This patient antiquarian wanders o'er
The heath, unsheltered, and in search of lore.

New light was thrown (though superstition
    spurns)
When he unearthed those rude primeval urns.
What time has passed since these men lived,
    ye seers ?
Say, is it two, or fifty thousand years ?
That theme I leave to-night.   I must pursue
Those rippling streams of crystal mountain dew.

Success to Swindon, Thursden, and Cant Clough !
Of faults and loamy clay, we've had enough.
From Shedding Top, and Bouldsworth's snow-
    capped hills,
The limpid currents dash in sparkling rills ;
From Gorple point, and down from Robin Hood,
Each valley pours a pure transparent flood.
The Muses never sweeter water drank,
Than Jockey Spring, which bubbles from the
    bank.
With streams like these I name, wide, deep, and
    clear,
And water from Cant Clough, we need not fear.
Let York and Chester laud their hills and dales,
We boast of scenes in our *Lancaster* vales.
When all those streams are tapped that
    clearly run,
No man need thirst along the banks of Brun.
Then let this town, *Lang-cast-(h)er* future hopes,
On Thursden's gushing streams and Shedding's
    slopes.
The Streets Department's health I humbly
    move;
Of all improvements some men disapprove.
This great committee makes your level streets,
Though some it leaves undone, and some
    completes,

Their labours often make them many foes ;
Fair play's a jewel, so the motto goes,
Though hard its duties, yet it ne'er exults,
Nor is it *Baron* either of results.
I know not who's to blame or who began it,
This awful row about Dalbeatie granite ;
I don't condemn its purchase, or excuse it,
But why not lay it in the streets and use it.
'Tis worse than madness, thus to go on raving,
The sets are paid for, get along with paving.

Success, long life, and if they want it, wealth
To that department, which secures us health;
'Tis true we've clean swept streets and spacious
               paths,
But wretched roads to our ill-lighted baths.
Your household refuse, too, is swept away
Without offence, before the break of day;
Who now permits a nuisance is a dunce,
And must be sent to *Keighley*, sir, at once.

That dull department, Sewage, comes the next,
The members of this branch may feel perplexed;
If gratitude is due, it is to those
Who kindly take a nuisance from our nose.
If well paved streets each district once secures,
With channels clean, and ventilated sewers,
All pipes and drains well trapped and throttled,
And all vile smells at Duckpits bottled ;
Where every nuisance and effluvium,
Shall rest in beds of pure alluvium.
If traps and pipes are not in good repair,
Then go and tell the man that *Burrows* there.

Through all confusion and through all
    mischances,
Good men we have obtained for our finances ;
Each cheque long may they honour at the call,
Like Higham's hindmost man they pay for all,
If you withhold your rates, you'll fare the worse,
And find a *Thorn-bur* sharply in your purse.

The town is also *Watched* and all within
Who now disturb the peace, will be run in,
Their guardianship we know, and thus accept,
How-arths and homes are now securely kept.

Our market branch has seen her troubles end,
Large profits now her useful work attend,
And those who break or injure any stall,
Must surely go to *Bailey* one and all.

The cemetery branch I name the last ;
This finds a home, to which we're travelling fast.
That final, purely democratic spot,
Where each man gets, of land, an equal plot ;
The good, the bad, the sordid, rich, and poor,
Must pass in solemn silence that dark door ;
Of all that's earthly each man gets his share,
And till the crack of doom he's *Holden* there.

TO THE CHAIRMAN OF THE NELSON LOCAL BOARD.

I thank you, my friend, for your kind invitation,
To dinners or luncheons I need no persuasion,
The courses, though many, are seldom too
    fulsome,
My system salutes them as kindly and
    wholesome ;

Then mark these few lines, that in rhyme I'm
    transmitting,
I'll turn up in time, and in garments befitting.
And now my friend Wilkinson, Nelson's good
    chairman,
At duty's high post, be impartial and fair, man;
The balance of justice hold firmly and meekly,
Yet if it incline, let it lean to the weakly.
May wisdom and truth be the stars of your
    guiding,
To steer the sage Board over which you're
    presiding;
May envy, and discord, and selfishness perish,
And Nelson, brave Nelson, still prosper and
    flourish.
Long life to yourself, and your wise Local
    Boarders,—
(With faculties free from all mental disorders),
Your sons, and your wives, and your daughters
    of beauty;
Like Nelson of old, may you all do your duty;
This prayer in conclusion, I fervently utter,
As thus I subscribe myself, friend, Harry Nutter.

A BURNLEY FISHERMAN'S SONG.

TUNE—'Derry Down.'

In Burnley, the pride of the Calder and Brun,
Ere Bruce with his license restrictions begun,
Two fishermen met at the Wellington Inn,
And fathomed a noggin of Nicholson's gin.
    Derry down, &c.

For rods or for swimmers they ne'er had a wish,
But both had a weakness for groping for fish ;
Old Joseph or Steven would far sooner die,
Than strike with a hook or deceive with a fly.
    Derry down, &c.

They called him a savage and void of all skill
Who pierced a poor innocent fish through the
        gill ;
Such arts they discarded, by river and pool,
And called Isaac Walton a cruel old fool.
    Derry down, &c.

Unsafe in their coverts were gudgeon or trout,
If Joseph and Steven were groping about ;
With dexterous fingers they stroked them all o'er,
Producing sensations they ne'er felt before.
    Derry down, &c.

Contentions arose as to which was the best,
At tickling a fish when asleep or at rest ;
These fishermen knew when the evening had
        closed
Where nightly the dear little fishes reposed.
    Derry down, &c.

The art of an angler a trout might defy,
With a worm covered hook or a treacherous fly ;
But could not the hands of these sportsmen
        elude
In the darkest recess where their hands could
        obtrude.
    Derry down, &c.

They tickled their bosoms, their sides, and their
    fins,
And chuckled them tenderly under their chins,
Then fondly they clasped them, and raised them
    on high,
They changed their condition, then calmly
    they'd die.
           Derry down, &c.

A challenge of skill by old Steven was made ;
On Joseph a guinea was instantly laid :
The wager was fixed and the poachers set out,
To tickle and capture the dear dappled trout.
           Derry down, &c.

The night was propitious, conditions allured,
The full harvest moon by a cloud was obscured ;
Old Calder flowed smoothly, the fish were well
    fed,
The watch-dogs and keepers were snoring in bed.
           Derry down, &c.

The fishermen ran to the banks of the stream,
Disdainful of danger, their vows to redeem ;
When Joseph announced that the game had
    begun,
The bell in St. Peter's tolled solemnly one.
           Derry down, &c.

Old Towneley's ancestral mansion was dark,
The timorous deer were alert in the park ;
The valley was silent from Dinely to Ridge,
When the contest commenced at the foot of
    Handbridge.
           Derry down, &c.

'One favour I'll grant you,' said Steven, 'for
    luck ;
Ten minutes a start you shall have in the brook ;'
Then Joseph rushed down to the water in haste,
So eager for sport that no time would he waste.
            Derry down, &c.

Each corner he tested with masterly hand,
While crafty old Steven remained on dry land,
And slily pretended to keep a look out,
To see if the keepers were lurking about.
            Derry down, &c.

'Here's a pool,' said old Steven, 'where often-
    times I
Have groped it alone, and got many a fry ;
Your fingers are nimble, your knowledge is
    great,
Experience has taught you to tickle and wait.
            Derry down, &c.

Just under this bank, Joseph, give it a feel,
It's a nice shady nook for a trout or an eel ;'
In vain Joseph groped, then began to despair,
He found not a fish under boulder or weir.
            Derry down, &c.

Then Steven's deep trick was beginning to dawn,
On Joseph, who forded the river alone ;
'Dear comrade,' said Steven, 'pray keep up
    your heart,
Just make a beginning, and then I will start.'
            Derry down, &c.

The fisherman trembled without and within,
'Are you satisfied yet?' said his friend, with a
    grin ;
But Joseph stood silent, disgusted and cold,
His nether lip dropped, when he saw he was
    sold.
           Derry down, &c.

Poor Joseph now sullenly gazed on his friend,
He saw the old barn where the contest should
    end ;
Dismayed and outwitted, he felt in disgrace,
While Steven, old fox, had a smile on his face.
           Derry down, &c.

' No fish have we caught,' Steven artfully cried,
' You cunning old carving-knife,' Joseph replied,
' The wager is mine, sir, and that you shall
    know,'
' Nay, nay,' answered Steven, ' we'll call it a
    draw.'
           Derry down, &c.

' It's a draw, I confess : Steven, lend me your
    hand,
And give me a lift, for I scarcely can stand ;'
But Steven held fast to a tree where he stood,
Or instantly he would have been in the flood.
           Derry down, &c.

' You seemed to pull hard, Joseph ; was it a slip ?
Or were you intending to give me a dip ?
Your game I perceived, brother—do not look
    gruff ;
One *draw* at a time, sir, is surely enough.'
           Derry down, &c.

Thus Steven addressed his friend Joseph, who
      sighed :
' Pray take this advice as a lesson and guide—
Whenever you enter a contest again,
Just measure your man by the weight of the
      brain.'
          Derry down, &c.

'Tis sweet to rejoice o'er a conquest complete,
But nobler, with grace to accept a defeat ;
Then let this cold lesson sink deep in your heart,
Don't enter the stream with a ten minutes' start.
          Derry down, &c,

OPENING OF THE TOWN HALL, BURNLEY.

OCTOBER 27TH, 1888.

With tuneful strains my simple lines infuse,
Thou dear reserved and fickle-hearted Muse ;
Enlighten me with thy poetic beam,
While here I ponder o'er this mighty theme.
With lofty thoughts my mind illuminate,
As on this glorious subject I dilate.

The stately building, Burnley's hope and pride,
This day the mayor her doors throws open wide,
With hand ungloved and massive golden key,
The willing lock obedient yields the way.
Omnipotent its power the gold maintains
On 'Change, in fine town halls, or holy fanes ;
With key of gold from Balarat in hand,
No earthly bolt such lever can withstand.

This potent metal locks the human heart,
And makes it pity-proof in every part ;
The gold-lined icy bosom tearless sees
A needy brother bending on his knees.
Yea, sires and grandsires feeble, worn and old,
Have sued in vain to sons with keys of gold.

As humble bards all selfish themes must spurn,
I to my subject once again return.
The glorious structure with its modest spire,
And noble front with stout and neat attire,
Where Burnley's loyal banner proudly waves,
Above the pillars and the architraves.
The cheerful four faced clock with tuneful
      chime,
Whose wheels will work with true sidereal time,
Will be a signal clear on every side,
By night and day a beacon and a guide.

Henceforth we dedicate this hall to those
Who must in faith administer the laws
Of this great empire, with unbiassed mind,
With justice stern, and mercy sweet combined ;
Like old Lycurgus wise of Spartan fame,
May equity well meted be their aim ;
Let no cold hearted, cruel Justice trench
Upon the sacred precincts of the bench,
Nor ever judgment once be guided wrong
By any luring lawyer's wicked tongue.
The deeply penitent with prayer sincere
May plead with hope for true compassion here,
And youthful sinners, who for grace implore,
Will go their promised way, and sin no more.

The cells below where pity seldom strays
(Where scamps unhanged resolve on better
  ways),
Are warm, and dry, and safely under guard,
And well-aired beds are there, though somewhat
  hard.
Some men, 'tis true, are dungeoned free from
  guile,
And rashly thrust below to durance vile ;
To cases such as these, our hearts have moved,
When clear the victim's innocence was proved.

The Corporation now I name with pride,
In whom the grateful burgesses confide ;
His worshipful the aldermanic mayor,
With badge and chain must take the central
  chair.
To right and left the aldermen are ranged,
Where confidential words are interchanged,
These portly gentlemen, with great respect,
And sage-like mien, support the mayor elect.
The common councillors before them sit
With due allegiance, and submission fit.
The chairmen of committees take the lead ;
Upstanding, they address the mayor, then read
The minutes of committee meetings clear,
Reporting good results throughout the year.
On matters of importance they debate,
Devising means to lower the borough rate ;
Retrenchment is their object, aim and end,
And on efficiency you may depend.
Your thoroughfares and bridges, streets and
  roads,
Are now complete, that nothing incommodes.
The gas is cheap and bright without compeer,
The water pure and soft, like crystal clear ;

No borough in the kingdom can bestow
Such perfect blessings, and with rates so low.
Then chime away, ye glorious Town Hall bells,
Ring out St. Peter with thy heavenly peals,
Ye bands assist with instrumental call,
And give a welcome to our new Town Hall.

DISSOLUTION OF THE ODDFELLOWS' CLUB, BARROWFORD.

The following lines were given on Saturday evening, December 11th, 1886, on the dissolution of the Oddfellows' Club, which had held its meetings at the ' Fleece Inn,' Barrowford, for nearly sixty years :—

Most noble grand, and past grandmasters, too,
And loyal vice, this night we bid adieu.
Ye grand provincial masters of the past,
This noble lodge, to fate succumbs at last.
The club you loved through many a toiling year,
Must close this night a useful, grand career.
As all things have an end beneath the sun,
So must our club, its mission now is done.
The Ward who safely kept the outer door,
With broad brimmed hat, alas ! we see no
          more ;
The Tyler's cheerful voice and kindly glance
Will never more his brethren's names announce ;
He'll welcome us no more with heart and hand,
Nor sign or password at the door demand.
We give no more the deferential bow,
Nor raise our willing fingers to our brow.
The costumes which our high officials wore,
Who graced those benches in the days of yore,

The gilded valance and the master's chair
Will soon be classed among the things that
      were ;
No sounds harmonious will fraternal ring,
Nor sacred mystic rites new pleasures bring.
In bygone happy years, good heavens, how long !
Since these old walls resounded our first song ;
This room where secret ties were knit secure,
Where no fantastic show could long endure.
At festive seasons long ago we joined
In councils sweet, in one firm bond combined.
'Tis true our club has reached its journeys end ;
To aid the poor, yet willing hands we'll lend—
Love mercy still, be generous, kind and wise,
Like brethren live in peace and fraternize.

Although our institution now is *nil*,
For all that's good we stand united still.
Clubs end like all things mortal in decay ;
So empires fall and kingdoms pass away ;
Conditions ever change, and we with them
Are doomed to fall, like branches from the stem.
May we, like wise and prudent men, resolve
To make the best of things as they evolve.
Be bounteous still, without the mystic line,
And emulate the days of auld lang syne.

ON THE DEATH OF A NEPHEW IN HIS 21st YEAR, NOV. 1, 1888.

In silence I entered the home of my youth :
    There death had again cast a gloom,
The lad that I valued for honour and truth,
    Was cut like a flower in its bloom.

A brother sat pensive and gazed in the fire,
    Depressed by affliction profound ;
His darling old mother, his sisters and sire,
    In sorrow sat weeping around.

The charming old fiddle lay mute in the case,
    The bow by its side was unstrung ;
The fiddler lay sleeping in death's cold embrace,
    Once noble, still life-like and young.

There close wept an angel attendant and ward,
    A loving companion and friend ,
Who cherished and nursed with a tender regard,
    The poor suffering youth to the end.

In solo, or trio, or in the full score,
    He cheerfully tendered his part ;
Those hands will, alas ! be responsive no more,
    To gladden his dear honest heart.

Attentive, acute, and refined were his ears,
    To music, to morals, and worth :
Those eyes that oft bathed in affectionate tears,
    Are closed to all things upon earth.

Those fingers which tunefully tempered the
      screw,
    And swept each melodious string
With timely precision, so graceful and true,
    Will nevermore harmony bring.

Alas ! that musicians should sicken and die,
    That draw out the heart-stirring tone ;
Alas ! that such merit and attributes high,
    Should perish in life's blushing dawn.

SUNG AT THE MAYOR'S DINNER, JANUARY 24TH, 1890.

TUNE—' St. Patrick was a Gentleman.'

Come, dear capricious, careless Muse,
  At this our festive season ;
My wayward mind this night infuse.
  With wisdom, truth, and reason ;
Ethereal flights to me are vain,
  I sing of deeds sublunar ;
When friendly themes engage my pen,
  My task is finished sooner.

The Council members we revere,
  Who nobly represent us ;
Since every man that labours here,
  Is sound and *compos mentis ;*
Take heed, ye striplings, young in years,
  To sages who are riper ;
Be honest in your various spheres,
  To those who pay the piper.

Ye generous mayors of by-gone days,
  Who filled your posts divinely,
Accept old Burnley's thanks and praise,
  From Palace House to Dinely ;
Departed souls of sterling worth,
  Heaven rest each honest spirit,
May those who still remain on earth
  Your mantles pure inherit.

Four noble mayors St. Peter's found,
  Who kept the town in order :
Four Wesleyans true, Armenians sound,
  Who cherished and adored her ;

Still one remains within the fold,
    Whose worth Old Time enhances,
With steadfast aim, he true and bold
    Adjusted our finances.

The Independents, firm in faith,
    Who sing the song of Balaam,
Sent Lomas, Massey (true till death),
    And gentle Scott from Salem ;
Young Brunswick is, what we adore,
    Firm as the hills of Sharon ;
For wisdom deep, and gospel lore,
    She Keighley gave and Baron.

Here let my Muse expand her wings ;
    Her flight must never falter,
While Thornber reads and Greenwood sings,
    By Bethel's sacred altar ;
In facts and figures Bethel shines,
    Illustrious in the nation,
From rule of three to Euclid's lines,
    And Jones's mensuration.

Be Thornber wise throughout his term :
    Regardless of each party,
To hold the Corporation firm,
    The graceless eight and forty ;
When aldermen on either hand
    Are restless and unruly,
Then let him shake the chastening wand,
    And force obedience duly.

The mayor of Burnley let us toast,
    His wife, his sons and daughters,
May all their foes, like Pharaoh's host,
    Be lost in troubled waters ;

Long may our mayor adorn the scene,
　Where good men sat before him,
And at life's close, with soul serene,
　Have great-grandchildren o'er him.

Hail, Bethel ! Burnley's mayoral shrine,
　Raise high your glorious standard ;
Hold firm the grip of grace divine,
　From which we all have wandered ;
For Bethel's good I breathe a prayer,
　For scholars, friends, and teachers :
Heaven bless her mayoress and her mayor,
　Her members and her preachers.

JOHN ENGLAND'S (NELSON) 74th BIRTHDAY.

This day brings your seventy-fourth year to an
　　　end ;
　Your leaf is not withered nor yellow :
Thus may you appear till you're ninety, my
　　　friend,
And then may your nature be mellow.

That you may have many returns of the day,
　When you shrieked your first salutation,
Is the wish of a friend, who implores that you
　　　may,
　Be blessed with a fifth generation.

When viewing our passage through life upon
　　　earth,
　In honest and keen retrospection ;
Of scenes daily changing, of mourning and
　　　mirth,
　How meagre is our recollection.

The years of our life, John, are three score
      and ten,
  Though Death with his scythe may oppose us ;
Yet this was the time once allotted to men,
  And sung by the patriarch Moses.—

At times men by reason of strength survive
      more,
  Yet deeper is ploughed every furrow ;
And years when extended to four or five score,
  Are mingled with labour and sorrow.

Man born of a woman, his seasons are few,
  He droops like a flower in the meadow ;
Of visions departed he takes a review,
  ' He fleeth also as a shadow.'

Job spoke of a shuttle in ages gone by,
  When Bildad upbraided him sternly ;
But Job never dreamt that a shuttle would fly,
  As swift as they now do in Burnley.

Your wedding I well can remember, old boy,
  Forget it, John ?   Can you ?   Oh, never !
So ardent in love and encompassed with joy,
  When Jinny cried ' England for ever !'

Hurrah for Old England, John England I mean,
  Heaven keep you in age from repining ;
May England's dear grandchildren's children
      convene
  To bless you in autumn's declining.

Your name is an anchor of hope, and a tower,
  As firm as the nethermost granite :
Long may it remain with its freedom and power,
  The pride of this whirligig planet.

In terms astronomical, long may you steer,
  With an eye to the plane of your orbit;
Due East be your flight, like Elijah the seer,
  And Satan himself cannot curb it.

TO MR. AND MRS. H. S. ON THEIR WEDDING DAY.

I wish from this morning, dear Herbert and
    Annie,
That you may be prosperous, cheerful and canny,
And through a long life of such pleasures be
    sharing,
That with the best couples you'll shine by
    comparing.
Be kind to her, Herbert, though not eulogistic,
And don't interfere much with matters domestic;
May Annie be always a dear little darling,
And both of you free from contention and
    snarling.
Let her by affection endeavour to sway you,
As Paul has commanded, she dare but obey you;
She's bound by this oath, this hymeneal fetter,
To do what you order her up to the letter;
And, Herbert, you swore and you promised to
    cherish,
So if you refuse you will certainly perish.
Let home be a point of attraction, the centre,
And Annie must greet with a smile when you
    enter;
But if in late hours you desire an expansion,
Even then she must smile when you enter your
    mansion,
Yet if in one matter to please her you're willing,
Don't ask how she spends every penny or
    shilling,

But take it from me that she'll do what she can, sir,
Let this be admitted without a back answer.
And now, my dear Herbert, one word in
    conclusion,
Excuse this impertinent, saucy effusion ;
As guardian I claim just a last observation
On this most important auspicious occasion ;
While you're in the honeymoon fondly caressing,
A warden thus gives his advice and his blessing ;
May angels of mercy their wings ever flutter
Around the young couple, thus prays Harry
    Nutter.

A CHRISTMAS SONG.

TUNE—'Bow, wow, wow.'

Old Time is on the wing, my boys, the world
    is all in motion :
We live in days of telegraphs, and rapid
    locomotion.
And Christmas comes but once a year : we'll
    give him kindly greeting,
And sing our merry songs to-night, at this our
    yearly meeting.
    And the toast shall be, 'Welcome, Merry
    Christmas and our jubilee.'

Ye men of comprehensive skill, whose know-
    ledge is expanding,
When learning scientific facts, keep clear your
    understanding,
Both mind and matter study well, with rigid
    perseverance,
But don't assail religious truths by foolish
    interference.
    And our toast shall be, Welcome, &c.

You say the moon creates the tides,—now is
    not that a wonder ?—
And some explain the wind and rain, the
    lightning and the thunder,
The great Gulf Stream some make their theme,
    monsoons and hurricanos,
And others speak of boiling springs, and earth-
    quakes, and volcanos.
    Still our toast shall be, Welcome, &c.

You talk of Afric's burning sands, her valleys
    and her mountains,
Her wondrous alligator lakes, and Nile's
    mysterious fountains ;
Burton and Baker, Speke, and Grant, were
    truthful, bold, and manly,
But all admire old Livingstone, and also brave
    young Stanley.
    Still the toast shall be, Welcome, &c.

Geologists assembled here are men of observa-
    tion,
Who fossils find of ancient things, mollusca and
    crustacean,
Ten million years they talk about, and pre-
    historic ages,
And Adam, Noah, and Abraham, they term our
    modern sages,
    Yet the toast shall be, Welcome, &c.

Astronomers among us too, who give us exposi-
    tions
Of comets, and of meteors, occultations and
    transitions ;—

Of stars and systems so remote, though heretics
 may cavil,
'Twould take a cannon ball from here ten
 million years to travel.
  Still the toast shall be, Welcome, &c.

Here men talk loud of railway shares, of pre-
 ference and Contangos,
Of scrip and consols, Three per cents, and what
 the Erie gang does ;
By Fisk and Gould how some were sold, which
 threw them in dilemmas,
Honduras bonds and Luxemburgs, Grand Trunks
 and faithless Emmas.
  Still the toast shall be, Welcome, &c.

We've one old prophet here to-night, a clear
 delineator,
A man well read in ancient lore, a true prog-
 nosticator ;
He tells of old Chaldean kings and many a
 Gentile nation ;
How Moses slew the Amorites, and Og the
 king of Bashan.
  Still our toast shall be, Welcome, &c.

He speaks of mighty men of old, who fought
 in fields of battle ;
How David killed a giant bold, and made his
 forehead rattle ;—
Relates how old Belshazzar drunk, and what
 his father fed on ;—
Foretells a conflict yet to come, that dreadful
 Har. Magedon.
  Still our toast shall be, Welcome, &c.

PART II.

John Cronkshaw is our host to-night, a man of
    reputation ;
He gives us to this Christmas feast a friendly
    invitation :
With well-spread board, fit for a lord, in
    courses there's redundance ;
The tables groan with good roast beef, and
    puddings in abundance.
    And the toast shall be, Welcome, &c.

Rich soups were served and seasoned well, good
    oxtail, hare, and turtle ;
Fat ducks were brought, whose rich perfume
    spread fragrance sweet as myrtle ;
And good roast geese and turkeys too (with
    sausage *in decorum*),
Well stuffed with onions, suet, eggs, green
    sage, and sweet marjorum.
    And the toast shall be, Welcome, &c.

Fresh hallibut and turbot too, with good cream
    sauce I'll mention ;
Boiled chickens, tender ham and tongue, all
    served with prompt attention ;
Red-currant jam and venison I do not care a fig
    for ;
The best of all upon the board was a little
    roasted pig, sir.
    And the toast shall be, Welcome, &c.

Potatoes, carrots, turnips, greens, and plants I
    cannot number ;
Asparagus and celery, pine-apple and cucumber.

We had custard made of cream and eggs, and
    some of Monmouth snow too,
And puddings, plum, and cabinet, and some of
    Tapioca, too.
    The toast shall be, Welcome, &c.

We had fine Italian jellies, and ribbon, I
    remember ;
Cheese, apple pies, and charlotte too, adapted
    for December ;
Delicious tarts, preserve and mince, fit for the
    queen Bellona ;
Apples, pears, and oranges, and nuts from
    Barcelona.
    And the toast shall be, Welcome, &c.

So now good night, my merry boys, the year is
    nearly ended ;
In that which is approaching fast, may all our
    lives be mended.
May memories of departed friends be a sweet
    and sacred treasure !
May health and peace and plenty flow upon
    you without measure !
    And the toast shall be, Welcome, &c.

SONG ON EVOLUTION.

TUNE.—'Jockey to the fair.'

*A discussion having taken place in Cronkshaw's
Hotel on 'Darwin's Evolutionary Theory,' the
following song was composed, and sung at a
Christmas party in the same place.*

As years roll round with rapid flight,
Each season brings some sweet delight,
The charming spring, the summer bright,
And autumn's golden hours.

And winter : what a grand array
Its lengthened frosty nights display ;
The silver moon, the planets gay,
The twinkling stars, the milky way,
    And meteors fiery showers.

And when the heavens are overcast,
And blinding sleet is falling fast,
Or Boreas blows his keenest blast
    In furious storms of hail.
When falling showers obscure the gate,
And starlings to the south migrate,
Then in this room wise men debate,
And people's rights they advocate,
    And bigotry assail.

Our festive night comes once a year,
When our good host gives welcome cheer
Let fierce discussion disappear,
    And harmony abound.
The kindly toast, the merry song,
The sparkling wit, the ready tongue,
The honest friendly feeling strong,
To Cronkshaw's happy tribe belong,
    And here true joys are found.

And now, that patience I implore,
Which you have granted heretofore ;
I'll sing of curious things of yore,
    Which some of you dispute.
Was man created from the dust ?
Is one great question here discussed,
For some this theory now distrust,
And say, forsooth, we really must
    Be offsprings of the brute.

They say the fossils still proclaim
The forms of life through which we came,
And give the history of our frame,
  By nature's wise decree.
Through every class, through every clan,
Through ages vast for proofs they scan,
To find how first our race began :—
The high antiquity of man,
  Our ancient pedigree.

No matter how obscure and strange,
This life's low germs evolve and change —
They each connecting link arrange,
  And every proof assign.
Though prejudice and pride demur,
The Ape was our progenitor :
That cunning thief, I tell you, sir,
Was our most gracious ancestor,
  Your grandpapa and mine.

While fossiliferous rocks remain,
And life's evolving forms contain,
Let wild fanatics rave in vain,
  The truth will still prevail.
Let Darwin every care bestow,
The true descent of man to show ;
How twenty million years ago
The monkey into man did grow,
  And how he lost his tail.

Now let me ask you to reflect
Before this theory you reject,
And treat the monkey with respect,
  And filial kindness too.

So, when the organ-grinders bring
That little ancient crafty thing,
Held by the collar with a string,
A copper, please, be sure to fling,
 As kinsfolk ought to do.

And now, my boys, once more adieu,
Our time is short, our pleasures few,
Let this our festive night renew
 The memories of the past :
And though we fail to comprehend
How life began, how life will end,
We still with adoration bend
To one great Author, Maker, Friend,
 Of power and wisdom vast.

GEOLOGICAL CHRISTMAS SONG.

DECEMBER 31ST, 1874.

TUNE—'Cork Leg.'

'Tis Cronkshaw's feast my pen employs,
So I must sing you a song my boys
At Christmas time, with all its joys,
When puddings and pies each man destroys,
 Ri too ral loo ral loo, &c.

When winter's whistling winds are bleak,
And bats and toads for shelter seek,
In some old wall or dismal creek,
'Tis then that pigs and turkeys squeak.

When in this room contentions cease,
We wave the olive branch of peace,
Though love and friendship still increase,
'Tis a terrible time for ducks and geese.

This is an age of enterprise,
When all false theories we despise ;
We really now are grown so wise,
That everything we must revise.

We've great philosophers here to-night,
Whose kind attention I'll invite,
For wondrous things I will recite,—
And tell how atoms re-unite.

This earth, we are told, was all gases at first,
And thus through its orbit for ages traversed,
Until by invisible power it was forced
To slowly condense, then the vapours
     dispersed.

Thus during these ages 'twas terrible weather,
When numberless particles, light as a feather,
Were whirling through space, and which nothing
     could tether,
Till forces molecular bound them together.

These primitive atoms, by law, aggregate,
Completely in time to their second estate ;
How strange that these gases should consolidate,
And crush and unite at a wonderful rate.

These atoms were pressed in a circular crowd,
All molten and glowing, and boiling aloud,
Then steam was thrown off in the form of a
     cloud,
And covered the earth with a vapoury shroud.

Now this is a theory that I have been told,—
Our globe in this state must for ages have rolled,
Until the hot surface began to grow cold,
And this is the doctrine that I shall uphold.

Some say at the first from the sun it was cast,
That Sol threw it off by a terrible blast :—
It then as a comet for ages was class'd,
And these are the changes through which it
    has pass'd.

In time, then, the primary shell of our planet
Was formed, when the gases condensed that
    o'er ran it ;
No doubt radiation it was that began it,
And now this first crust is most beautiful
    granite.

But ere I begin from the base to ascend,
The minerals I'll name that these rocks
    comprehend,
They are mica and feldspar and quartz and
    hornblende,
And granite's the mother of rocks, I contend.

Then the series they call the Laurentian rocks
Come next, which contain life's original stocks ;
And this I am told, that these primitive blocks
Were rent and upheaved by Plutonian shocks.

Now the next crust above the Laurentian zone,
Is the tilted and useful old Cambrian stone ;
These primary rocks a great thickness had
    grown
You'll now understand, for in Wales they are
    shown.

Just above is the lower Silurian bed,
Where traces of life are perceptibly spread ;
And rivers, and seas, and huge tempests have
    sped
For millions of years o'er the living and dead.

Though the upper Silurian series consist
Of rocks, where the fossils of zoophytes exist,
Yet most of the vertebrate fishes are miss'd,
All this I am told by the geologist.

So now I must leave the Silurian strand,
Where forms of the crustacean Trilobite stand,
And rise to the rocks of Devonian sand,
With fish in the oceans, and trees on the land.

Then limestone, and grit, and the coal beds
          obtain,
Where ferns and the Lepidodendron remain,
On which the whole Permian system has lain,
For millions of ages, some people maintain.

I still proceed upwards, and looking around
Where fossils of plants and strange insects
          abound,
And where the Marsupial Mammals were found,
And hideous reptiles crawled over the ground.

I pass many other strange groups on my way,
The Liassic, Oolitic, and chalk I survey,
Till at length I arrive at the London clay,
And all the strange forms of the Tertiary day.

The next group above are the crags Coralline,
And just over that is the group Pliocene,
Where the Till of the Clyde, and crags
          intervene,
And primeval man near the surface is seen.

If time would allow of great wonders I'd sing,
And tell how strange creatures from others
          might spring;
Of lizards and vampires and bats on the wing,
When forests with huge roaring monsters did
          ring.

Of glacial action and storms long ago—
Convulsions, and drifts of whole mountains of
      snow ;
Of earthquakes, volcanos, with terrible throe,
Where land was upheaved, and where land slipt
      below.

And now, in conclusion, I beg to remind you
That seventy-four you are leaving behind you ;
May the year seventy-five invariably find you
Enjoying good health, with good temper com-
      bined too.

SPIRITUALISM—A BURLESQUE.

Sung at Cronkshaw's Christmas Party December,
28th, 1876.

TUNE—'There is no Luck about the House.'

The world still moves around, my boys,
    And seasons come and go,
And health and pleasure in their turn
    Must follow pain and woe ;
Though war, and crime, and ignorance,
    May scourge us for a time,
Yet happy days we have in store,
    I'll prove it in my rhyme.

The changes that have come about
    Within a few short years,
Will set your troubled minds at rest,
    And dry your foolish tears.
The greatest wonders of the past
    Are nothing now indeed,
Compared to those we hear of now,
    I'll prove as I proceed.

The doctors hence will have no work,
   And no one will complain,
For mediums will cure us all
   Of every cursed pain.
Young office boys take my advice,
   And learn another trade,
For spirit guides will do your work,
   Through Monck and Doctor Slade.

The soothsayers of the present day
   Have surely lost the spell,
And dark-eyed Spanish gipsy girls
   No fortunes more will tell.
Though Pendle Forest witches once
   On magic broomsticks flew ;
Demdyke and Chattox are eclipsed,
   And the witch of Endor too.

The prophets who prognosticate
   Of famines, plagues, and wars,
Astrologers who wisely rule
   The planets and the stars,
And shrewd magicians of the past,
   Who answered Pharaoh's call,
With mediums of the *present* day,
   Could not compare at all.

Our fathers all desired to see
   The great men of the past,
And, lo ! the mystic mediums
   Have found them out at last ;
Then on a table lay your hands,
   Just as the medium begs,
The spirits soon will flock around,
   And run about your legs.

The spirits come by magic force,
  And some by sleight of hand,
They tap and turn the table round,
  And answer each command ;
Though spirits pass the shades of death,
  And peaceful rest obtain,
Professor Monck and Dr. Slade
  Can bring them back again.

From distant climes the spirits come,
  Though some are very near,
A few are brought against their mind,
  Yet others volunteer ;
The spirits walk around the room,
  And sing behind the screens,
Whilst others play the fairy bells,
  And some the tambourines.

The spirits come from east and west,
  The friend as well as foe,
From purgatory some are torn,
  And others from below ;
Though all the powers of earth and air
  May firmly hold their grip,
When Slade's enchanted hand is raised
  Old Satan lets them slip.

Now when the tables move about
  These wondrous things I'm told—
That you can have an interview
  With marvellous men of old ;
One evening lately such a host
  Of friends came in a crack,
The Caliph of Bagdad, Old King Cole,
  And the Prince of Sarawack.

And two great souls dropp'd in also,
   By the medium's high command,—
Bold Robin Hood and Little John
   With bow and arrow in hand ;
The medium urged the forester bold,
   Whose darts were bright and keen,
To empty his quiver of fatal shafts
   On Cook and Maskeyleyne.

Some true-born Irishmen came next,
   Bedecked in colours green,
Saint Patrick danced a jig, and sang
   The wedding of Ballyporeen ;
And Scottish chiefs in native dress
   With plaids of each design,
Will Wallace gave the Highland fling,
   And Bruce sang Auld Lang Syne.

Next came Llewelyn, Prince of Wales,
   Of whom each Welshman boasts,
Who proudly dared King Edward's power,
   With Cambria's valiant hosts.
He sang the song of Harlech men,
   Who never would be slaves.
Then last of all brave Nelson sang
   " Britannia rules the waves."

John Gilpin and Jack Horner came,
   Dick Whittington with his cat,
Giles Scroggins and Dame Durden too,
   Dan Tucker and Jack Spratt.
King Dick and Nicodemus called
   As they were passing through,
And Nebuchadnezzar came with them,
   And Robinson Crusoe too.

Will Watch and Black-eyed Susan came,
    With Joe, the poor marine,
Kate Kearney brought the Minstrel Boy,
    And sang "God save the Queen."
The Lass of Richmond Hill was there,
    And a pretty girl was she,
And Nancy Dawson introduced
    The Miller of the Dee.

The kindly spirits come alone,
    Though some will bring a mate.
And others even write a verse
    With pencil on a slate.
But just before I close my song,
    Which mediums will condemn,
I warn them to be careful, lest
    The tables turn on them.

So now adieu my boys again,
    May pleasure be your lot,
Whilst memory holds her seat with me,
    You'll never be forgot.
And when the storms of life are past,
    And each his part has played,
May none of us e'er be disturbed
    By Monck or Doctor Slade.

MAN AND THE APE.

Tune—'The King of the Cannibal Island.'

Come list to what I've got to say,
Whilst our relations I survey,
I'll prove to you as clear as day
That man is akin to the monkey.

Down in the deep Laurentian stone,
The protoplastic germs were sown,
Which formed the simple eozoon,
From which all living things have grown ;
The ancient rocks beneath contain
A true and clear connected chain,
The intermediate links explain
How man has evolved from the monkey.
   Then look at your lineal pedigree,
   The gorilla, or gibbon, a brother may be,
   The orang-outang, or the chimpanzee,
   Or some other pithecus monkey.

From fish and flesh descending through
Amphibia, snakes, and reptiles too,—
The vampire and the kangaroo,
Before you arrive at the monkey ;
   And when the struggle for life arrives,
   The best developed oft survives,
   And thus the fittest form deprives
   Ill-favoured creatures of their lives.
The varying forms and species strange,
In grand transitional order range ;
By fresh conditions all must change,
Both fish and fowl, and monkey.

   Then look at your lineal pedigree, &c.

These proofs successive ages find,
From divers groups of mammal kind,
That man is but an ape refined,
So never despise the monkey.
   His restless cunning eye bespeaks,
   That he some artful mischief seeks,
   His gambols are like boyish freaks,
   With his dimpled chin and whisker'd cheeks.

Like us vile passions they display,
And surely you will not gainsay
That, when your children disobey,
You call them little monkeys.

    Then look at your lineal pedigree, &c.

When paths of rectitude they leave,
And unto bad companions cleave,
Like us the miscreants sometimes grieve,
And turn repentant monkeys.
    But when their violent passions rise,
    They scream and scratch each other's eyes,
    Like mortal men they tyrannise,
    The strongest will the weak chastise ;
Like boys they roll in fits of rage,
And direful conflicts sometimes wage,
When only death can disengage
These little wicked monkeys.

    Then look at your lineal pedigree, &c.

They nurse their children, helpless things,
The mother rocks, and hums, and sings,
And o'er her shoulder sometimes swings
The little infant monkeys.
    Like Christians sometimes blessed with twins,
    And when the suckling time begins,
    They clasp them close beneath their chins,
    And kiss their hands and stroke their skins.
They place one gently to each breast,
And nestling fondly by them pressed ;
When washed and combed and neatly dressed,
They scarcely look like monkeys.

    Then look at your lineal pedigree, &c.

By human plagues their infants droop,
Convulsions, chicken pox, and croup,
And measles take at one full swoop
A tribe of delicate monkeys.
　　Like children too the young ones weep,
　　And during teething miss their sleep,
　　A constant watch their parents keep,
　　And round their suffering offspring creep.
But when their children droop and die,
With sorrowful lip and tearful eye,
And piteous wail and bitter cry,
They mourn their poor lost monkeys.
　　Then look at your lineal pedigree, &c.

Just look at his fatherly form and face,
How much he resembles the human race,
No great distinction you can trace
Between the man and the monkey.
　　The proud may sneer with haughty pride,
　　And bigots too may snarl and chide ;
　　The truth I'll tell whate'er betide,
　　They're only monkeys modified :
Then don't deny your brotherhood,
The fossils prove the kindred stood,
A million years before the flood,
So never disown the monkey.
　　But look at your lineal pedigree, &c.

NEW INVENTIONS.
Tune—'Dumble Dum Dearie.'

'Tis pleasant to gather each year, and behold
The wonders which nature and science unfold :
Truth, reason, and error, huge conflicts have
　　waged ;
Traditions and falsehoods with science engaged :

Old legends must wane,
But truth will remain,
Though dark superstition may ne'er be assuaged.

Could visits be paid by our fathers, to view
The past and the present, the old and the new,
A blessing they'd deem it to live at this day,
When the strongholds of bigotry yield and decay,
When science sheds light,
False theories take flight,
And stupified prejudice stands in dismay.

We are told that the spirits of evil conspire
To torture and dip us in brimstone and fire :—
That Satan would chuckle to see us in pain,
And, serving us right, would eternally chain
Us in darkness and gloom :
This pitiless doom
Would be ours and thus we should ever remain !

But, thanks to those parsons who preach to us
now,
Who cast off false dogmas and honestly vow
That the Scriptures of old no terrors contained ;
But hell and its agonies priests had ordained :
They put on this threat
In order to get
Our wicked and obdurate natures restrained.

So now we are taught that the Father above,
Whose justice is tempered with mercy and love,
Will look with compassion on Adam's poor heirs,
Consider our natures, afflictions, and cares,
And when He begins
To look up our sins,
Will think of our passions, temptations, and
snares.

What mighty inventions this age has unfurled !
Lo, telegraph wires now encompass the world ;
The regions of darkness are well nigh explored,
And distance and time are completely ignored ;
    To the uttermost clime,
    In a moment of time,
A definite telegraph message is scored.

Through telephones, lately invented by Hughes,
You'll bring every sound to your homes if you
    choose :
If stormy the weather, you need not despair,
You'll listen to sermons at home in your chair.
    And if you desire,
    To chant with the choir,
You thus at a distance the worship will share.

When sick, and the doctor great care
    recommends,
You'll sit by the fire with your wife and your
    friends ;
Connections of wire with the pulpit you'll keep
When sermons are long, or the subject's too
    deep,
    You will be justified,
    And the parson won't chide,
If by chance you quietly drop over to sleep.

But where it will end there's not one of us
    knows,
This telephone now may each secret expose—
Each whisper in private, by damsel or swain—
And even the innermost thoughts of the brain,
    Which now are concealed,
    May soon be revealed,
And all our mysterious deeds be explained.

Our naturalists now may all listen with glee,
To the song of a midge, or tramp of a flea ;
Their coughing and sneezing be heard, and each
    groan ;
And the signs of buzzards and butterflies known.
    When sick or in grief,
    They will ask for relief,
And our natural sympathy then may be shown.

The phonograph, too, is a wonderful thing ;
Repeating the words they may utter or sing ;
A song or a sermon which anyone hears,
May turn up again, when he likes it appears.
    Each familiar word
    By his friends may be heard,
At the lapse of many long troublesome years.

To friends at a distance, the phonograph may
Assist correspondence, in this simple way ;
Enclose in your letter the tinfoil you use,
And friends any time can the sounds reproduce,
    The identical voice
    That will make them rejoice ;
Their pleasure in future will thus be profuse.

Thus many advantages yet may be found,
By means of repeating and transmitting sound ;
What joys you may reap with this talking
    machine,
Any night when a number of friends you
    convene.
    It will whistle or sing
    Any tune that you bring—
" The last rose of summer," or " God save the
    Queen."

But the greatest discovery I mention the last,
Oil, candles, and gas lamps are things of the
    past !
For a light is invented, so brilliant and pure,
That the dazzle of noonday may always endure.
      Then never repine,
      For each village will shine,
No matter however the place be obscure.

In future this charming and wonderful light
Will luminate cities and towns in the night.
From Pendle, and Boulsworth, and Hambledon
    Hills,
You'll light up the valleys, shops, houses and
    mills.
      The light is so keen,
      All points will be seen,
For every corner with brightness it fills.

These lights will be beaming from mountains
    and towers,
And darkness unknown in this island of ours.
In vain will the stars try to brighten the scene—
The blaze of the planets will scarcely be seen,
      And our neighbour, the moon,
      Which has long been a boon,
Will seldom, if ever, be noticed, I ween.

And now, my dear boys, I must bid you adieu,
Of recent inventions you've got a review,
To you that are upright these things have a
    charm,
But lovers of darkness may feel some alarm ;
      For the deeds of the night
      Will be brought unto light,
And virtue be certainly shielded from harm.

THE BURNLEY WATER SCHEME.

TUNE—'O dear, what can the matter be.'

Two years ago, when this borough was flourishing,
Hopes in the future, the Council was cherishing;
Some one announced that we soon should be
    perishing,
What could the jeopardy be !

CHORUS :

O dear, what can the matter be,
Dear, dear, where can the water be ;
What will become of old Burnley's posterity,
What will they do for their tea ?

The Council's position was not very pleasing,
The water was scarce, and the Borough increas-
    ing,
Improvements required their attention unceas-
    ing :—
And bothered for money were they.
    O dear, what can the matter be, &c.

Engineers were engaged, whose worth we might
    count on,
To fly to the hills and examine each fountain :—
To measure the sheddings, each valley and
    mountain,
And on a good site to agree.
    O dear, what can the matter be, &c.

The valley of Swinden had surely not done ill,
Yet Emmott would take Robin Hood through
    a tunnel ;
And pour into Swinden his stream through a
    funnel,
And mix it with one, two, and three.
    O dear, what can the matter be, &c.

Wise people would make down the hill a conduit,
Old Burnley they ventured to say would not
    rue it ;
The water from Robin would gravitate through
    it,
    And pass by the side of the Lee.
      O dear, what can the matter be, &c.

The prospects of Stephen, though distant and
    gloomy,
Its natural basin is rounded and roomy ;
They falsely report that the clay is all loamy,
    Alas ! what will engineers say ?
      O dear, what can the matter be, &c.

This truth you will learn, that wherever you
    travel,
That proud engineers are accustomed to cavil,
They say that Old Stephen is troubled with
    gravel,
    His water will never be free.
      Oh dear, what can the matter be, &c.

'Tis said that his water when boiled in a kettle
Will turn rather milky and canker the metal,
When clay in suspension refuses to settle,
    What will your grandmothers say ?
      Oh dear, what can the matter be, &c.

John Sagar then asked Mr. Filliter's pardon,
And firmly maintained, and would venture his
    word on
The water being pure in the streamlet of
    Jordan, —
    And limpid as water could be.
      Oh dear, what can the matter be, &c.

John Williams protested against the expenses,
And also proclaimed that a man in his senses
Had only to look at the walls and the fences
   For proofs that the surface would stay.
      Oh dear, what can the matter be, &c.

The speeches of Heap and of Riley and Taylor
Proved clearly that Filliter's scheme was a
    failure !
The Mayor in his robes then began to look paler
   And tapped the Town Clerk on the knee.
      Oh dear, what can the matter be, &c.

The Burnley Town Council now thought it a pity,
Yet sympathised much with the Water Com-
    mittee,
They all were determined that this future city
   Should have a good water for tea.
      Oh dear, what can the matter be &c.

F. Hargreaves the chemist (whose aid was
    requested)
Then bottled the waters, and filtered, and tested,
And by his analysis he manifested,
   Which was the best water for tea.
      O dear, what can the matter be, &c.

The lovers of Stephen, though not very clever,
Consented at last from the valley to sever :
But yet they will love it for ever and ever.
   Though fate gave another decree.
      Oh dear, what can the matter be, &c.

Farewell to New Bridge, Robin Hood, and old
    Stephen,
Hell Clough and Jerusalem too we are leaving,
For thee, little Jordan, I also am grieving,
   Your beauties no more shall I see.
      Oh dear, what can the matter be, &c.

James Emmett resolved that his mind he d
    unfetter,
Then slipped off to Leeds about Filliter's letter,
And brought out a scheme that he said would
    be better,
    And offered his plan without fee.
        Oh dear, what can the matter be, &c.

Now Filliter soon fell a sighing and sobbing,
When learning the news of the meeting on
    Robin.
In summer they scarcely could water old
    Dobbin ;
    A dearth there would certainly be.
        Oh dear, what can the matter be, &c.

Wiseacres seemed but to chuckle and laugh
    again,
Came to their senses, and then they went off
    again,
Then at the wise engineers they would scoff
    again,
    How could they ever agree ?
        Oh dear, what can the matter be, &c

We now bid adieu to the banks of Jerusalem,
The tunnel and Bridge, we have fairly got loose
    of them,
Then drink from Cant Clough till your old like
    Methusalem ;
    Three cheers for our bright jubilee.
        Oh dear, what can the matter be, &c.

I hope you will pardon this silly effusion,
Which now I must bring to a hasty conclusion ;
May all your discussions be free from confusion
    At this Eighty-two Jubilee.
        Oh dear, what can the matter be, &c.

A CHRISTMAS SONG

TUNE—Fine Old English Gentleman.

When days are short and nights are cold, and
cruel roars the blast :
In winter's frost, or driving snows, old Christmas
comes at last.
When local quarrels, doubts and fears, are all
behind us cast,
When honest men shall meet no foes, but friend
to friend stand fast.
At this our Christmas festival, one of the
present time.

No scorn, malignity or pride, can flourish in
this place,
For every welcome comrade here beams with a
smiling face :
Let recitation, toast and song, keep moving on
apace,
And let us all be merry, boys ; nor think it a
disgrace.
At this our Christmas festival, one of the
present time.

Of rare profession we have men, and men of
title too,—
Solicitors and chemists wise, and doctors not a
few,—
Engineers and loom makers, and blacksmiths
in our crew,
With other men of metal keen, who make the
bolt and screw.
At this our Christmas festival, one of the
present time.

We've book-keepers and managers, who are not
there misplaced,

And men who make good peppermint, and
    pop to suit your taste ;
Firm pickermakers, paper hangers, sizers with
    their paste,
And men of reputation high, who deal in fly
    and waste.
    At this our Christmas festival, one of the
      present time.—

In earthenware we have, who deal in fire-brick,
    pipe and pot,
And architects, and stationers, and masons we
    have got ;
With ironfounders, tinners too, and joiners in
    our lot,
Cabmen, and undertakers grave, but sextons we
    have not.
    At this our Christmas Festival, one of the
      present time.

Collectors smart and clerks we have, who claim
    each local tax,
And gard'ners and greengrocers, with potatoes
    in their sacks ;
Sharp tailors, grocers, drapers clean, and
    hawkers with their packs,
And butchers, skinners, tanners brown, and
    cobblers with their wax.
    At this our Christmas festival, one of the
      present time.

We've men who manufacture cloth, and some
    who spin for gain ;
Shrewd agents and good salesmen too, for fancy
    goods and plain :
A clear-voiced bellman, deep and wise, with
    penetrating brain,

And one who makes velocipedes, and all things
    can explain.
    At this our Christmas festival, one of the
        present time.

And yet, ere I conclude my song, if you will
    tolerate,
About this motley company some other things
    I'll state—
Of bakers, painters, readers, poets, whom we
    venerate,
And men of engineering skill, who prove and
    demonstrate.
  ·   At this our Christmas festival, one of the
        present time.—

Geologists, zoologists and botanists of fame,
And titled physiologists, who understand our
    frame ;
Photographists, biologists (and mesmerists I'll
    name),
And one old wise evangelist of true prophetic
    flame,
    At this our Christmas festival, one of the
        present time.

My song is ended now my boys long may
    your hearts be light,
Let song, and glee, and speech go round this
    merry festive night ;
May Cronkshaw's children live in peace and
    never have a blight ;
Our host and hostess now we toast, let each
    man stand upright.
    At this our Christmas festival, one of the
        present time.

CHRISTMAS ASTRONOMICAL SONG.

TUNE—'Bow-wow.'

This wicked world still onward flies, and
   measures out a year, sir ;
And spinning as she steers away, throughout
   her wild career, sir ;
Like cannon shot she flies along, still on the sun
   depending,
And wings her utmost speed to-night, just when
   the year is ending.

Though changing speed as on she flies, she keeps
   her true position,
And finishes her yearly race to time with true
   precision ;
But yet the year is not complete, till nearly six
   to-morrow,
Then every leap year you contrive to pay back
   what you borrow.

Oceans and clouds adhere to her, as on her path
   she courses,
Mid thunder-storms and earthquake shocks, and
   all sublunar forces,
As through ethereal space she flies, persistently
   she's turning,—
And gently in those merry rounds produces
   night and morning.

The happy seasons come and go with kindly
   variation,
In consequence of one great law : the polar
   inclination ;
O'er twenty three and half degrees, she bows
   unto her orbit,
As on through space she takes her flight, where
   nothing can disturb it.

This night I dwell on mighty themes, and
theories deep unravel,
I'll tell you at what speed you fly, as round the
sun you travel ;
This planet's path is well defined; she keeps
exactly in it,
And thirteen hundred Irish miles, she flies in
every minute.

Did she one moment stop her flight, the shock
would be unpleasant,
Like wax this ponderous globe would melt to
matter incandescent ;
Ye sages, raise your prayers on high, and
ardently petition,
That this dear planet never pause, or fly in
swift collision.

Empires and kingdoms all would end with every
institution,
Old Pendle would that moment be in fervent
dissolution,
The pyramids, Mount Ararat, and Sinai and
Hermon,
Would fall with all their ancient lore, each
sacred book and sermon.

But things are not just what they seem, indeed,
I'll try to prove, sir,
The moon inconstant though she is, all honest
people love her :
Although she gaily shines by night, in haughty
pride and splendour,
Her light, she borrows from the sun, as much
as he will lend her.

Though Cynthia seems to wax and wane, and
    hide her features from us,
Or spiteful steal behind the clouds, and unto
    darkness doom us,
She undergoes no lunar change through her
    capricious phases,
But casts reflections from Old Sol, as on the
    earth she gazes.

The flaming source of light and heat that
    brightens the horizon,
That millions daily worship and devoutly fix
    their eyes on ;
It seems to fly from East to West, and never
    once relaxes,
'Tis but the earth, though turning round, upon
    her silent axis.

The sun is not where he appears, to our terrestrial
    vision,
We see him where eight minutes prior, he took
    his true position ;
The stars in yon sidereal vault, that glitter on
    so brightly,
They are not where they seem to be, although
    you see them nightly.

Light flies along at lightning speed, and this is
    duly reckoned,
Two hundred thousand English miles it travels
    in a second ;
Light takes a hundred years and more (on this
    you may rely, sir),
To come from stars that you can see, with
    unassisted eye, sir.

The stars of heaven are numberless, and space is
    deep and endless,
I'll leave you on the threshold there, but not
    entirely friendless ;
And now good night, once more, my boys, may
    blessings rich betide you—
And all your stars be lucky stars, that will to
    fortune guide you.

MICHAEL THE BRAVE.

TUNE—'Derry Down.'

In a Barrowford dandyshop, long, long ago,
On the banks of the clear Pendle Water below.
When the salmon and trout graced the silvery
    stream,
And the shuttle was pickt through the shed
    without steam.
    Derry Down, Down Die Derry Down.

Each weaver was busy at work in his loom,
When an Irishman, frantic, rushed into the
    room :
"Who struck Paddy Kelly ?" he asked with a
    frown.
" By Jabus I'll crack in a moment his crown."
    Derry Down, &c.

"For vengeance I came; I am Michael the brave
Whoever smote Pat must prepare for his grave
The rascal shall know that I'm famous in deeds ;
No truce will I make, while a counthryman
    bleeds."
    Derry Down, &c.

(A mighty shillelagh he waved in the air,
And eyed every weaver with menacing glare:)
" The man who struck Paddy must meet me in
    strife
The divil a chance there will be for his life."
        Derry Down, &c.

His coat he threw down in a terrible rage,
Saying show me the man that will Michael
    engage ;
The villain at once I will seize by the throat,
If he will but step on the tail of my coat.
        Derry Down, &c.

Then down on his coat thundered big Barley
    Jack,
Mick saw his dimensions, then stepped a pace
    back ;
Down dropped his shillelagh slap bang on the
    floor,
When he saw that big Johnny had bolted the
    door.
        Derry Down, &c.

With horror poor Michael the giant surveyed,
Then fell on his knees and for mercy he prayed ;
But Jack bared his arm and prepared for the
    fight,
' By gorra," said Michael, " you served the fool,
    right."
        Derry Down, &c.

" Pick up your shillelagh," said Jack with a
    smile,"
" Ye witty and dexterous cunning old file :
Your heart is too tender, your head is too wise,
To fight with a man nearly double your size."
        Derry Down, &c.

" You're a gintleman, sur," answered Michael at
    once,
" Bad luck to Pat Kelly, the coward the dunce,
The spalpeen I know is a quarrelsome elf,
When I meet the young rascal I ll bate him
    myself."
        Derry Down, &c.

In toiling through life, to this counsel attend,
Give faithful and earnest support to a friend;
Take Michael's advice, 'tis an excellent plan,
Before you do battle, just measure your man.
        Derry Down, &c.

ANSWER TO AN INVITATION
TO A PARTY.

Your kind invitation came duly to hand,
    Though very untimely for me ;
Far off on that date in a beautiful land,
    Your friend will undoubtedly be.

I'm sorry dear sir, thus to hasten away,
    From dinner, from friends, and from home ;
But when you are feasting this sinner will pray,
    And send you his blessings from Rome.

You'll think, though, when toasting in pleasure
    and hope,
    In friendship's most affable grip,
That I may be kissing the toe of the Pope,
    With a curl on my nethermost lip.

Should I in St. Peter's with Romans convene,
    To bend on apostasy's knee !
The toe of the Pontiff, no matter how clean,
    Would not receive kisses from me.

Bright eyes must dictate with a passionate glow,
What words ever fail to express ;
And joys the most sacred, dear lips must bestow,
Both pilgrim and Pope must confess.

TO Dr. BURNS ON HIS SILVER WEDDING DAY.

I wish you most fervently many returns
Of your dear silver wedding, remember ;
Your love for each other still ardently *Burns*,
On this twenty-first day of September.

It seems but a season, sir, since she was young,
When the ring on her finger was shaking,
And you were high-swearing with promises
strong,
To the beautiful girl you were taking.

You say that you never had cause to regret,
Or a fear that your passion might falter,
This twenty-five years, since the day that you
met
Her, before the Hymenial Altar.

Still may you be sturdy and buoyant on earth,
And not from her pleasures with-holden,
May long rolling years give you comfort and
mirth,
Until the grand wedding day-golden.

Then on may you laugh with your darling old
wife,
Still may she obey your kind bidding ;
May grand children's children, then bless you
through life,
And attend at your diamond wedding.

There's a genuine charm in the name that you
  bear,
Pure, electric, acute and refined,
That name will ring on everlasting and fair,
A rich blessing, and boon to mankind.

TO MR. C., ON RECEIVING A BRACE OF PHEASANTS.

Your messenger came to my cottage this
  morning,
With a radiant smile on his face ;
Two pheasants his generous hands were
  adorning,
A beautiful dear speckled brace.

My gratitude turned to a feeling of pity,
  When viewing their plumage of gold ;
Their poor broken pinions and bosoms so pretty,
  Afflicted my heart to behold.

The glossy young birds, though, were juicy and
  tender,
And plump as dame Nature could bring ;
Especially that of the feminine gender,
  In brisket, leg, kidney, and wing.

Accept my best thanks for the lusty, delicious,
  Oviparous, vertebrate pair ;
That fortune to you may henceforth be
  propitious,
Is the humble recipient's prayer.

AN ELEGY ON EDWIN WAUGH.

Grim Death, old Nature's ancient foe,
Has winged a shaft with fatal blow,
And laid a darling poet low,
    Whom we deplore :
The harp of dear old Edwin Waugh
    Will sound no more.

Ye local bards, whose music rings,
When fanned by dialectic wings,
Your homely Muse now vainly springs,
    And deeply grieves :
Hang up your harps and drape the strings
    In Cypress leaves.

Permit a poor North-eastern bard,
Whose Muse is feeble and ill-starred,
To thus express his deep regard
    And reverence,
For one, whose verses seldom jarred,
    Or gave offence.

Thee, Waugh, alas, no more we see !
But, wherefore say alas for thee,
From pain and trouble now lies free
    Thy manly frame,
And Waugh henceforth, will ever be
    An honoured name.

No squeamish culture mars his lines,
Nor pride fastidious e'er confines
His vein of wit, or undermines
    His merry theme :
In fireside stories there he shines
    In fun supreme.

His Barrel-organ's cheerful trill,
And Besom Ben, are with us still,
His songs of love our valleys fill,
        And ring on high :
The fruits of his Parnassian quill
        Will never die.

Two bards stood by his sacred bier
Who long had loved their great compeer,
And will his honoured name revere—
        While here below :
The name to them was ever dear,
        Of Edwin Waugh.

Ben Brierley's trembling feet, and slow,
Walked round the poet's dust below,
His genial face betrayed deep woe,
        And silent grief—
Whose silvery locks now clearly show
        The yellow leaf.

Sam Laycock paced the sacred place,
With anguish written on his face,
A genuine sorrow you could trace
        Upon his brow :
This tuneful dialectic brace
        Are lonely now.

These brother bards with ringlets gray,
Placed on his dust two garlands gay :
But on the turf their tears display
        What love bequeaths :
These signs fraternal far outweigh
        A thousand wreaths.

Farewell, dear Waugh, thy genial smile
Broad beamed in Nature's happiest style,
Thy books will tedious hours beguile,
    For years to come :
Though Death will soon thy brethren file
    To their long home.   ·

TO Mr. WILLIAM CHRISTIE, THE REAL SCOTCH MINSTREL,

On his Silver Wedding Day, Sep. 30th, 1890.

The theme of my verses, dear Christie, old friend,
    May be seen by the style of their heading ;
Just twenty-five Summers have rolled to an end,
    Since the day of your bright happy wedding.

That fortunate morning, my dear Scottish boy,
    With delight you will ever remember,
Which promised long years of connubial joy,
    From that thirtieth day of September.

Man's life is a puzzle, a blessing or curse,
    For unquenchable pleasures he's sighing :
But when he takes woman for better or worse,
    A most dangerous path he is trying.

Yet blessed is the man who secures a good wife,
    (Though a bachelor always is dreading),
But dearer by twenty-five times is her life,
    On the morn of her grand silver wedding.

With love for your wife may your bosom still
    flame—
And be free from all worldly temptations ;
Still long may you cherish and bless the old
    dame,
    At least through a fourth generation.

Sing on as each season Autumnal returns,
  Sing of Wallace, of Bruce, and of Charlie ;
Sing on, the sweet songs of your own poet,
    Burns,
  Scots Wha Hae, and the dear Rigs O'Barley.

Your voice to a circle of friends is a boon,
  Of your songs we shall never be weary—
Bonnie Jean, and the waters of Afton and Doon,
  Mary Morison, and Highland Mary.

Your children, dear branches, that honour the
    stem,
  May each one be a boon and a blessing ;
And, Christie, my boy, may you still honour
    them,
  When their children you're fondly caressing.

Throughout a long life may your heart remain
    soft—
  Keeping clear of all wicked Philistines ;
When closing life's scenes, you will all soar aloft,
  For your wife, and your children are *Christians*.

LONG SERMONS.

A little boy, named Simeon Pratt,
Late in a Burnley temple sat,
One dull autumnal Sabbath day,
Passing his youthful time away ;
No text or subject could he tell,
Nor did he like the sermon well ;
His face betokened deep dismay,
And still the parson preached away.
The lad was tired and sighed to go,
His nether lip was hanging low,

With anxious aspect, I suppose,
He prayed that soon the book might close.
An hour and more at School he'd been,
His appetite was growing keen ;
In pain he sat, his limbs being pent
In undeserving punishment ;
The teacher would not let him sleep,
Although his yawns were loud and deep.
Poor Simeon's visage seemed to say,
Oh, close the book, and sing and pray.

Fat Jacob Swires and Jonas Moor
Had fallen twice upon the floor ;
Their little knees and feet and shins,
Were pricking like a thousand pins.
Sylvanus Ward and Isaac Towers,
With cunning and mischievious powers
Were twisting William Turner's hair,
As he sat jaded, sleeping there.
Both boys and girls were tired I saw,
And so were we in pews below.

Ye who in lengthy sermons deal,
Pray hear a local bard's appeal ;
Recall the days when you were young,
And then restrain your tiresome tongue.
Let darling girls and noble boys
Have ample time for youthful joys,
Confine them not, I crave in rhyme,
As if they'd done some awful crime.

These youths (for whose release I speak)
Are toiling hard throughout the week ;
Each day half time at school and mill,
Of work and precept get their fill.
Observe what high extatic bliss
Thrills through their souls when you dismiss.

Lastly, brethren, now supposing
We combine for early closing ;
Urging each denomination
For a closer condensation.
If united, we determine,
For a twenty minutes' sermon,
Then the children—bless their faces,
Would sit smiling in their places.
Preachers would, in acquiescing,
Then receive a children's blessing.

In conclusion, let me mention,
No one pays the least attention,
To your sermons long and serious,
For they vex and often weary us ;
But to poor imprisoned children
Such discourses are bewildering :
English, Irish, French or German,
No one likes a lengthy sermon.

———

FROM BURNLEY.

In Celebration of Mr. Alderman Scarr's Fifty Year's Residence in Leeds.

All hail, fair Leeds, with Mayoral badge and
    gown,
Permit a stranger from a neighbouring town
To share your joys on this auspicious day,
And to your host his grateful homage pay.
Let no discordant jealous feelings mar
Your bliss with your good townsman, ex-Mayor
    Scarr.
Her greetings, Burnley sends to you this night,
And hails this great event with keen delight,

This night, in merry song and heartfelt toast,
She joins with your fair hostess and your host :
Thus Burnley on the Brun, her feelings share
With Leeds, upon the classic banks of Aire,
Here in this vale Scarr passed his youthful
hours,
And from our town he turned his steps to
yours :
Friend Scarr on Burnley looks with love and
pride,
For there he sighed, and wooed, and won his
bride.
With joy long may he retrospective muse,
Upon the day that sealed the nuptial noose.
'Tis meet that Leeds and Burnley thus respond
In this fraternal, generous, social bond.
With honest pride long may his host relate
The fact, that fifty years before this date
He placed his youthful feet—tired, trembling,
sore—
Upon the very threshold of your door,
And how he toiled the busy crowd among,
With steadfast aim, and resolution strong,
Through all these changing years, with anxious
care,
Till Leeds awarded him the civic chair.
Success must crown the youth who runs and
reads,
And emulates friend Scarr's career in Leeds.

THE TURKISH ATROCITIES.

There arose from the East a loud cry o'er the
sea—
'Twas the wail of the poor wretched slave to be
free ;

Twas the weeping of infant, and mother, and
    sire,
And the shrieks of the victims rose higher and
    higher.
Shall the maids of Bulgaria for help vainly cry,
And the nations of Europe stand silently by ?
Let the proud flag of England defend us, they
    pray,
Or depart with your vessels from Besika Bay.

Lo, the dastardly monster slays widow and bride,
When your uplifted finger would stop the red tide;
And such deeds are allowed which we blush to
    record,
When a menace from England would sheathe
    the vile sword.
Sure the sight of each victim, and unburied
    skull,
Will proclaim the Turk's cup of iniquity full ;
Then arouse, mighty England ! your influence
    display,
Or else pull down your standard in Besika Bay !

Shall the bold and the generous true sympathy
    shirk
Whilst violence and murder are wrought by the
    Turk ?
Shall the ag'd and the infant be sabred and shot,
And their fate be ignored, unavenged, or forgot ?
Shall the tars of Old England, the brave and
    the good,
Protect hideous fiends whilst they revel in blood?
Shall the tigers and wolves fill the world with
    dismay—
With the flag of Old England in Besika Bay ?

CHRISTMAS SONG ON CO-OPERATION.

TUNE—'The Rakes of Mallow, or
Bobby Shakky, O.'

PART FIRST.

As time rolls on and years expire,
When snows the leafless trees attire
We gather round John Cronkshaw's fire,
    And never disagree, sir;
It is our custom you perceive,
To take a final, friendly leave
Of passing years, on New Years' Eve,
    At Cronkshaw's jubilee, sir.

While plodding through life's little span,
Let each one here do all he can
To cheer and help his fellow-man,
    By wise co-operation.
That times are good, you're all agreed;
I'll sing of schemes as I proceed,
With profits large, and risks indeed
    Have all a limitation.

Each morning's early news consists
Of railway stocks and shipping lists,
Of mining shares, where wealth exists,
    And how each market ranges;
Of Yankie bulls, and English bears,—
Egyptian funds, and canal shares,
And Chillian bonds, and Buenos Ayres,
    And all the stock exchanges.

What mighty wonders we behold,—
How stocks and shares are bought and sold,
And every project rings with gold,
    Without the least disguising ;
We've broker's journals once a week,
With information that you seek,
From Sandy Gate to Cedar Creek,
    And every land comprising.

Now all prospectuses denote
What grand concerns there are afloat,
If you don't buy a joint-stock vote
    You'll be quite isolated ;
If you will search the borough through,
Of joint-stock mills you'll find a few ;
We've got some paper makers too,
    Who are incorporated.

Hill Top and Oxford Mills are seen,
And Olive Mount and Keighley Green ;
And Crook and Collinge too I ween,
    Are profitable spinners ;
Each tradesman now co-operates
With lawyers and with magistrates ;
The parson too confederates
    With publicans and sinners.

We've card machines with maker's names,
And drawing, slub, and roving frames,
All tended well by trusty dames,
    Who walk the alleys proudly ;
Dead mules are moving to and fro,
Sweet throstles sing the winter through,
With pretty girls to feed them too,
    And devils roaring loudly.—

New looms for fancy goods and plain,—
Sateens and drills, and good twilled jean,—
Fine shirtings wide, and stripes for Spain,
    And heavy goods for winter ;
The madopolam and common T,—
The jacconet, and small dhootie,
We also hold supremacy,
    For Mexican and printer.

PART SECOND.

Co-ops. we have for selling tea,
A Burnley Carriage Company,
And ironmongers too I see,
    With chimney-piece and fender ;—
In Burnley's handsome market place,
And just beneath the large clock face,
Where Sheffield goods the windows grace,—
    Of modern style and splendour.

They here supply all minor trades
With silver spoons and delving spades,
And pocket knives with Rogers' blades,
    And plated knives and forks too.
Good drills and files for artisans,
And garden rakes and watering cans,
And dripping tins and frying pans,
    With stomach pump, and corkscrew.

There's everything upon the rack,
Both pans and kettles painted black,
The toddy spoon and bottle jack,
    And papier machie waiters ;—
Steel gimlets, saws, and planes and rules,
And various kinds of joiners' tools,—
Strong iron stands, and kitchen stools,
    And mops and nutmeg graters.—

Bright cruet frames to suit your wives,
And buck-horn handled table knives,
And patent earthenware beehives,—
    And troughs for cattle graziers ;—
Strong jockey bars, and larding pins,
Fine jelly moulds and pudding tins,
And lather brushes for your chins,
    And shaving pots and razors.

They've shovels, pokers, tongs, and rakes,
And oven tins for pies and cakes,
And iron grids for frizzling steaks,
    And mincing pots and beaters.
A patent steel with ivory hand,—
A handsome nursery basin stand,
And cans and canisters japanned,
    And warming pans and heaters.—

Light slop pails, cans, and copper cones,
And small machines for mowing lawns,—
Good Brunswick black and rotten stones,
    And blacking paste and bootjacks ;
They've cocoa, tea and coffee urns,—
A useful toasting jack that turns,—
Plates, dishes, butter knives, and churns,
    And curling tongs and nutcracks.—

Flour bins, weights, and family scales,
And water pipes and water pails,
And locks and bars, and bolts and nails,
    And warming tins for cradles ;—
Fine corner dishes, green and blue,
And sugar nippers, choppers too,
And porridge pans, and some for stew
    And basting spoons and ladles.—

Strong wardrobe hooks for cloaks and caps,—
Brass kettle stands, and water taps,
And mouse, and rat, and rabbit traps,
    And hammers, vice, and gauges.—
Rich Toilet sets, and iron cots,—
Grand iron bedsteads, and what-nots,
And porridge spoons, and mustard pots,
    And parkin-cans, and cages.—

Good barrel taps, and copper pegs,
And silver spoons for salt and eggs,
And carving knives, and jackolegs,
    And clipping shears for fleecemen ;—
Bright lanterns, lamps, and candlesticks,
And hammers, levers, spades, and picks,—
Handcuffs for thieves and lunatics,
    And bulls-eyes for policemen.—

Fine gasaliers, of bronze and brass,
And smart reflectors, lined with glass,
And cooking stoves prepared for gas,
    Of every new invention.
Time won't allow me to define
How use and ornament combine
In articles of high design,
    Too numerous to mention.

And now to all assembled here—
Long may our friendship be sincere,
Long may this house provide good cheer,
    And never harbour treason ;
Long may our generous host prepare,
On New Year's Eve, a sumptuous fare,
Long may his wife and daughters share,
    The pleasures of the season.

A NEW YEAR'S ADDRESS.

To Mr. C. M. Foden, Hon. Secretary to the Mechanics'
Institution, Burnley.

Dear Foden, our grand Institution, you make
  Her service your duty, though large ;
Her business you know, and with joy undertake,
  In strict honest faith to discharge.

With pleasure, now twenty-two years I review,
  Your patience, industry and care ;
In duty so zealous, obliging and true,
  From weariness free, and despair.

Exertions most noble have made you revered
  In meeting, and concert, and ball :
To teachers and scholars you're truly endeared,
  And loved, and respected by all.

Your word is as true as divinity's scroll,
  Your purpose is never disguised :
Your bosom is blessed with an untarnished soul,
  In labours of love exercised.

For our Institution, you see what's required,
  Yea, every want, and appliance ;
The classes you furnish with all that's desired,
  In technical arts, or in science.

The masters you prove, and secure us the best,
  You challenge the haughty inspectors ;
Against all extravagant schemes you protest,
  As checker, and guide to directors.

Reports you submit, all accounts you compile,
  Read out, criticise and explain :
When passed and discounted, you place on a file,
  They then in your archives remain.

Newspapers and telegrams quick you provide,
　For Burnley's grand Royal Exchange :
And chemicals, basins and bottles beside,
　For work in each class you arrange.

When funds are depressed, and requirements
　　encroach,
　You never forsake her in trial ;
Her friends for　subscriptions　you　kindly
　　approach,
　And never will brook a denial.

Our　mayors, lords, and gentry, you　humbly
　　beseech,
　To open their ponderous purses :
More　power to　the donors, who fill　up　the
　　breach,—
　Supplying what Foden disburses.

All matters artistic with pencil or paint,
　In this Institution are rife :
There pupils may practice with little restraint,
　Fine drawing and painting from life.

For languages foreign, Dutch, German or French,
　Provision most ample is made :
For teachers and scholars on every bench,
　All books for their service are laid.

For ladies, specific arrangements are found,
　And kitchen utensils are brought :
For lessons domestic provisions abound,
　And all kinds of cooking are taught.

All courses of study for those that compete,
　Are well with preceptors supplied :—
Geology, botany, sound, light and heat,
　And others not here specified.

If one man has earned the best wishes of all
   Directors, and wards, and trustees,
'Tis you honest Foden that answers the call,
   On this every member agrees.

The thousands of pupils at home and abroad,
   Who now are enlightened adults,
Will bless their friend Foden with tears over-
     flowed,
   For labours with glorious results.

At last, let me name the great efforts combined,
   Of Foden and Alderman Scott,—
Your dear predecessor, so gentle and kind,
   Whose mantle you certainly got.

These few broken lines, though but faintly
     impart,
   The feelings my thanks are bestowed in :
Yet freely they're poured with a fulness of heart,
   To you my dear friend C. M. Foden.

No vain adulation my Muse will conjure,
   No flattering favour express
To one so deserving, unselfish and pure,
   Whose value no man can assess.

In service by day, not a moment you waste.
   Your duties are never neglected ;
You're trusted by those that are over you
     placed—
   By those who are under; respected.

Work on, my dear Foden, your labours will tell,
   And benefit ages to come :
Long may you in honour and harmony dwell,
   To bless this old town, and your home.

TO Mr. A. STANSFIELD,
KERSAL MOOR, MANCHESTER.

Hail, brother bard, with cultured brain !
Your lines in Scotch have made me vain ;
You should not speak so strong and plain
  Of what you feel,
For you're so powerful with your pen,
  And versatile.

I doubt not that your honest heart
Felt keen and warm in every part ;
But men like you, who are so smart,
  Should be *mair tentie,*
And shed less kindness at the start,
  Although you've plenty.

You pour your brilliant, tuneful flame
Too freely (though with friendly aim) ;
For this, my boy, you're much too blame,
  And I must grumble ;
Your city friends had prior claim
  To one so humble.

Friends Tam and Geordie I admire,
And well I know each fine strung lyre ;
My feeble Muse could not aspire
  To their dominions ;
They sweeter sing, and soar far higher,
  On stronger pinions,

With mundane things I'm so beset,
That with you three I've rarely met ;
But every time we closer get
  I'm more enlightened ;
The future may bring leisure yet,
  With raptures heightened.

Could we arrange, say, once a week,
To spend an hour just check to check,
And blithely sing, or freely speak,
    And form a set,
My Muse would join (though poor and meek)
    In full quartette.

I'd friendly chat with you in turns,
On poets' works, and what concerns
Great Dante, Shelley, Byron, Burns,
    Goldsmith, and Keats ;
To hear of these my spirit yearns,
    And thus entreats.

A social evening now and then
Our minds would burnish, we might ken
The imperfections of each pen,
    And meet as brothers ;
Pray write (and fix the place and when),
    And bring the others.

Adieu, my genial friend, once more !
Your heart is noble to the core ;
In foreign deep linguistic lore,
    You're eminent ;
Had I your knowledge well in store,
    I'd be content.

SONG.—OLD BETHESDA.

TUNE—' Afton Water.'

I'll sing of Bethesda, the pride of my youth,
The shrine where is taught the sweet gospel of
    truth :
Though poor is her flock, and her Church
    unendowed,
Yet here our dear forefathers piously bowed.

Thy service, Bethesda, is modest and pure,
Thy tenets are sacred, and so must endure ;
Thy dear hallowed story with joy we enrol,
Thy temple, Bethesda, is dear to my soul.

Thy school where on Sundays the youths gaily
    throng,
Whose walls once re-echoed our infantine song,
Is now inconvenient, unhealthy and old,
Its days are all numbered, and soon will be told.
Thus temples and schools upon earth must decay,
In life's evolutions the old pass away :
The school of our parents will soon disappear,
Yet fondly we love it, and long will revere.

Bethesda, the sacred, true faith's pioneer,
Thou church where each Sabbath glad tidings
    we hear,
Thy pulpit is famous for freedom of thought,
Advanced are thy doctrines, and fearlessly
    taught.
Thy teachers and pastors whose names we still
    love,
Are gone to sweet mansions of pleasure above,
We love thee, Bethesda, thou dear holy shrine,
Sweet memories around thee eternally twine.

INDEX.

www.ingramcontent.com/pod-product-compliance
Lightning Source LLC
Chambersburg PA
CBHW020017030726
47500CB00002B/637